10 Bodies Lying
(a Body Movers novel)

STEPHANIE BOND

"A man is never more truthful than when he acknowledges himself a liar." —Mark Twain

CHAPTER 1

Carlotta WTF? Wes told Chance UR holed up in the townhouse, won't say why. Call me.

Hi dear… me again… I'm so sorry for what I did… to you… and to your father. Can we talk?

Hi sweetheart… your mother is worried. U should call her. I hope U know how much we both love you.

Carlotta this is your little sister Priscilla texting you from Birch's phone because you will not answer your phone when I call you. If I had my own phone I could text you myself. All my friends have their own phones. I need you to take me shopping for a new dress for Amanda Gibson's pool party. Mom is crying a lot.

Yo, Sis—was thinking of making short ribs for dinner, just us, let me know. U can't stay in your room 4ever. It's downright Hitchcockian.

This is a message from the Fulton County Correctional Facility for: CARLOTTA WREN. You have been approved to receive limited, monitored text messages from: INMATE PETER ASHFORD. Reply OK to proceed or STOP to opt out.

Hi there… your mom's neurologist asked me to sit in on her appt yesterday, surprised u weren't there. Sorry if I made things awk between us. We can still be friends.

Hey... u haven't caused me overtime hours lately, everything ok?
How's Prissy & her puppy? We should talk sometime.

"CARLOTTA WRAN?" a male voice asked.

Carlotta looked up from her text messages. She was the only person in the waiting room. Still, she nodded to the tall, thin man wearing a sweater vest and bowtie. "Wren," she corrected, then pushed to her feet.

"I apologize, Ms. Wren," he said with a nervous smile.

"No worries," she murmured, thinking how ironic the man had gotten her last name wrong—evidently she'd gotten it wrong her entire life. "You must be Dr. Denton."

He looked startled. "Of course I am. Right this way." He extended his arm to invite her into his office.

Feeling out of place, Carlotta shouldered her bag and walked past him. As she scanned the room—stark, but well-appointed, the knot of anxiety in her stomach tightened. She never thought she'd be talking to a shrink, although anyone who knew much about her life would dub her a therapist's dream.

"Sit anywhere you like," he said, gesturing toward a triangle of two chairs and a couch. In the corner sat a simple desk, gently cluttered—very proper, very affirming. She gave him a little smile. "Do patients actually lie on the couch? I thought that was only in the movies."

"Some patients prefer it. I sometimes lie on it myself." Her expression must have reflected her puzzled reaction because he back-pedaled. "Only to nap, of course." He cleared his throat. "Can I get you something to drink? Water, coffee?"

"No, thank you." She glanced between the two chairs, which were identical except for the color—white and black. She paused, wondering if the psychologist would infer something about her by the chair she chose. Did one represent lightness and the other darkness, and was a person more likely to choose the color that represented their current situation, or the one that represented where they wanted their life to be?

She opted for the white chair in deference to her yellow Bella Tu dress—she didn't want to pick up black lint.

2

Dr. Denton folded himself into the other chair, armed—strangely—with a Hello Kitty notebook and pen. He gave her a pleasant, encouraging smile.

She crossed her hands in her lap, then uncrossed them. Her fingers itched for a cigarette—her nemesis habit was back with a vengeance. The silence stretched on. "I've never done this before," she offered.

He gave a dismissive wave. "Well, thankfully, I have."

Obviously he was trying to make her more comfortable, but she was starting to have second thoughts about spilling her personal traumas to a complete stranger. She glanced toward the closed door.

"Thanks for coming in during the lunch hour," he said, cutting into her thoughts.

"I appreciate you working me in on such short notice," she murmured, and tried to relax. The Wrens had agreed to try family therapy to learn how to communicate, but with the latest curve ball, she'd decided to seek out on her own psychoanalysis. She wasn't feeling a connection yet, but she wanted to give Dr. Denton a chance.

Still, her nerves danced as she waited for a sign to begin the session. When none seemed forthcoming, she asked, "Is there a protocol for starting?"

He shook his head. "Nope."

"So I should just… start talking?"

"Sure." Then he checked his watch. "And not to rush you, but we have to be finished in forty-five minutes."

"Oh." She shifted. "Okay… where should I begin?"

He shrugged, then held his pen to the notebook, as if he were poised to transcribe everything she said. "Why don't you just tell me what's bothering you?"

She couldn't hold back a bitter laugh. "How about everything?"

He made a mark in his notebook. "Can you be more specific?"

"Okay." She took a deep breath. "When I was a senior in high school, my parents skipped town so my father could avoid going to jail for a white collar crime. My brother Wesley was nine, so I had to raise him—and myself. It was tough… but we

3

managed. Then a few months ago, ten years after he went missing, my father was apprehended."

"Where?" he asked, scribbling furiously.

"Here in Atlanta. Actually, he came out of hiding to save me from being attacked by a serial killer."

Dr. Denton looked up. "Seriously?"

She nodded. "Wes and I were moving bodies for the morgue at the time, and it landed me in the middle of some messy situations."

His gaze flitted over her, head to toe. "You don't look like someone who moves bodies for a living."

"It's a side gig."

"And how does one become a part-time body mover?"

"Wes got me involved... and I guess Coop kept me involved."

"Who's Coop?"

"Wes's boss for a while, and mine. Coop works at the city morgue. He's... great." Her cheeks warmed.

"This Coop—he's more than a boss, I take it?"

She bit into her lip. "I thought so... more than once. But our timing is always off." Then she smiled. "My real job is with Neiman Marcus." Her recent promotion and the upcoming trip to Dallas was a bright spot on the horizon.

"Neiman's? *That* I believe." He pointed to her shoes. "Are those mules Alexander Wang?"

Carlotta blinked in surprise, then glanced down to the black and silver shoes. "Why, yes, they are." Admittedly, the man had good taste. And upon closer observation, his cufflinks were Gucci. *Nice.*

"Go on," he urged. "You were saying your father was arrested?"

"Yes. And while he was in jail, I found my mother. She was ill with what we thought was dementia. My father had hid out to protect her... and the daughter they had after they left Atlanta."

He glanced up. "So you have a younger sister you didn't know about?"

She smiled. "Yes. Prissy is nine... she's the best thing that's happened to our family."

He nodded and jotted. "So your father's in jail?"

"No." Carlotta exhaled. "As it turns out, my father isn't a criminal after all—his own partners at an investment firm set him up to take the fall for a massive counterfeit and money laundering business. He was exonerated and now they're all in jail, awaiting trial." She pressed her lips together. "Including my fiancé, Peter."

"Fiancé?"

"*Ex*-fiancé, I should've said."

He angled his head. "So why didn't you?"

She lifted her shoulders in a slow shrug. "I guess I'm still getting used to me and Peter not being a couple. He was my first love. We were engaged when my parents disappeared, then he broke it off."

"Ouch."

She squinted—the man seemed a little judgmental... but maybe this was a modern style of therapy? "It hurt at the time," she admitted. "But then he came back into my life and we were giving our relationship a second chance."

"Until he committed a felony?"

Carlotta frowned. Was he trying to provoke her? "I didn't break off our engagement because of the charges. I believe he tried to do the right thing, but he got caught between loyalties. We just weren't right for each other anymore."

He looked dubious, and made a note.

"My friend Hannah told me I got engaged because I was reacting to Jack being unavailable," she admitted.

"Jack?"

"The police detective who arrested my brother and was hunting my father." She squirmed. "Jack and I had an on-again, off-again... and on-again and off-again... thing."

"Had?"

She sighed. "He got another woman pregnant."

"You really know how to pick 'em, don't you?"

That stung. She wasn't sure if she was going to like Dr. Denton's therapy style, but she forged on. "Turns out the woman was a vile person who lied about the baby—not that her lying lets Jack off the hook. And even if Hannah was right about me turning to Peter on the rebound, I don't want Jack, even if he is available... and no matter what he was going to tell me."

The pen stopped. "What was Jack going to tell you?"

"I… don't know. He only said he hadn't told me things when he should have."

"What do you *think* he was going to tell you?"

"I… wouldn't guess." A big, fat lie, but no buzzer sounded.

"Is that why you're here? You're trying to choose between the men in your life?"

Carlotta frowned. "No. I mean—yes, I'm trying to sort out my personal life, but that's not why I'm here."

"Okay." He looked back to the notepad. "You mentioned your mother is ill?"

"Actually, we found out my mother doesn't have dementia after all. She's receiving treatment and hopefully she's on her way back to good health." Another miracle.

He lifted his head and smiled. "So all's well that ends well?"

She squinted. "Er… not exactly."

"Okay, then." He glanced at the clock. "Keep going."

She tried not to feel slighted—the man did have other appointments, probably with long-standing patients. "We've had a rough time finding our places as a family again—especially my dad and Wes. He was a boy when my parents disappeared and I don't believe Randolph understands Wes is a man now."

"Randolph?"

"Our… father."

He continued to write. "Go on."

"But we were on a better path… until we opened our Christmas presents last week."

"Christmas presents at this time of the year?"

She gave him a flat smile. "My parents disappeared right before the holidays, and my little brother refused to open the gifts until we were all reunited."

He leaned forward. "What was in the gifts?"

"Most of them were of little consequence," she said, then reached up to touch the pendant at her collarbone. "But my mother gave me this locket."

"Pretty. A family heirloom?"

"I suppose. She put a picture of my father inside."

"I take it you're close to your father?"

"I was before they left," she admitted. "I always thought Randolph and I had a special bond." She absently opened the locket and stared down at the photograph.

"May I see?"

She leaned forward, then turned the locket so he could view the tiny likeness.

He smiled. "Randolph is handsome."

"Yes," she agreed. "Except this isn't Randolph. Apparently, this is my real father."

"Oh." One eyebrow rose. "You didn't know Randolph isn't your real father?"

"No."

His other eyebrow went up, then he covered his mouth with his hand. "No shit?"

Carlotta voice faltered. "Er... no."

"And do you know the man in the picture?"

"No."

"Wow. How are you dealing with it?"

"Not well," she admitted dryly. "Which is kind of why I'm here."

"Oh... right," he said, then seemed to gather himself. "What can I help you with, Carlotta?" He glanced toward the clock, then back.

She lifted her hands. "I guess I'd like to know why everyone lies to me."

He frowned. "That's a blanket statement, don't you think?"

"But it's true," she insisted, then counted on her fingers. "My parents lied to me my entire life... Peter lied to me... so did Jack. Wes has lied to me too many times to count. My friend Hannah lied to me about her background and her family's connection to Randolph. Even my coworker Patricia took the job at Neiman's just to inform on me to the District Attorney."

He pursed his mouth. "In my experience, people who don't tell the truth usually have a good reason—have you ever tried to look at it from the other person's perspective?"

She squinted. "Um... no."

"Think about it—if you're convinced everyone you meet lies to you, you're the common denominator. Maybe you're the problem, Carlotta." Dr. Denton sat back in his chair, looking triumphant.

Carlotta's mouth parted in surprise—wasn't therapy supposed to be a judgment-free, safe place to open up? While her mind raced to process a myriad of mixed emotions, the door behind them opened.

Carlotta turned to see a paunchy, graying man wearing a sportcoat standing in the doorway. In one hand he held a sack of takeout food. He surveyed the two of them with a cautious expression. "George, what's this all about?"

Across from her, the bow-tied man sprang to his feet. His face turned a mottled red. "Dr. Denton... you're back from lunch early."

"And who is this?" the man at the door asked, giving her a tentative smile.

Carlotta looked back and forth between the two men, dread building in her stomach.

"This is Carlotta Wran," George offered magnanimously.

"Wren," she corrected, pushing clumsily to her feet and away from the man she'd been talking to. "If you're Dr. Denton," she said to the man at the door, "who is this?"

"George is one of my patients," the doctor said quietly. "What did you do, George?"

"I was just... taking some preliminary notes for you," George stammered. "She's a good one, Dr. Denton—her life is a soap opera." Then he put his hand alongside his mouth, as if to impart a secret. "She thinks people lie to her. Personally, I thinks she's paranoid."

Carlotta was backing away, mortified she'd just told her life story to a complete stranger—a mentally unstable stranger.

"I apologize, Ms. Wren," the doctor was saying as she passed him. "I don't know how this happened, but I promise you—"

She didn't wait to hear him out. With her heart hammering, Carlotta jogged back through the waiting room and into the hall. After stabbing the elevator button, she opted for the stairs and scrambled down them faster than was probably wise. When she burst into the building lobby, people moved out of her way. She race-walked out into the parking lot, but was running by the time she reached her car. She fumbled for the keys, then swung inside

8

the stifling interior, slammed the door, then locked it. She turned over the engine and put the air conditioner on high, then lit a cigarette with shaking hands, squashing the scream that lurked in the back of her throat. Worse than the crazy man's deceit—yet more lies—was the fact that he'd unwittingly identified her greatest fear.

Maybe you're the problem, Carlotta.

She inhaled until her lungs were ready to burst, then blew a cloud of white smoke into the air.

Minus ten points.

CHAPTER 2

WESLEY WREN checked his phone to see if he'd missed a message from Carlotta—he never thought he'd see the day when he wished his sister would talk *more*. But since their mother had dropped the bomb that Randolph wasn't her biological father, he'd scarcely heard three words out of her. He'd been eager for her to move back into the townhouse, but not under these circumstances.

It was still agonizing to think of the day they'd been opening their gifts left under the tree ten years ago, celebrating being reunited as a family now that their mother was well enough to participate. Things had been going well—his parents and his sisters were so happy. Then Carlotta had opened the necklace from their mother... and everything had changed.

He lifted his hand to stab his glasses higher, then found a tiny bit of fingernail that wasn't yet bitten into the quick, and gnawed on it until he felt the flash of raw pain indicating he'd gone too far. He lowered his throbbing finger and checked his phone again— maybe Meg had texted.

But no.

He sighed. The two most important women in his life were for all intents and purposes MIA—Carlotta had holed up in her bedroom at the townhouse, and Meg Vincent was in Germany for the summer. Right now she was probably drinking huge warm beers in a bawdy biergarten surrounded by beefy guys hoping to get into her tight American jeans.

He pulled his hand over his mouth. The bag of Oxy pills he'd bought a few weeks ago from a guy in the park were still in the freezer, suspended in a block of ice... but it was getting harder to ignore their call.

Only the threat of a weekly urine test from his probation officer had kept him straight.

"Wren!" the crone at the window shouted. "You're up!"

He pulled himself up, then stopped as he walked by the frumpy, grumpy woman and leaned on the ledge. "I know you only treat me like crap because you have a crush on me."

She rolled her eyes up to him. "Move it, smartass, or I'll crush something alright."

He blew her a kiss, then ambled toward E.'s office. At her door he stopped to sniff his pits, decided he didn't reek, then lifted his hand and knocked.

"Come in," E. said.

He opened the door and acknowledged a lift to his mood—and to his nuts. With Meg gone, he hadn't had a pretty woman around to look at.

E. Jones was sitting at her desk, but had leaned over to remove a file from a drawer. Her pink blouse had fallen forward to reveal a lighter pink bra, with a little embroidered flower in the middle of her cleavage.

He loved the bras with the little flowers. Meg had a drawer full of them.

When E. cleared her throat, he glanced up at her pointed look and blushed. *Busted.*

"You can have a seat, Wes."

He lowered himself into the chair opposite her and waited.

She straightened and opened his file, then crossed her hands. "Tell me what's going on with you."

He shrugged. "I'm good."

She studied him, then nodded. "Your community service for breaking into the courthouse database is nearly finished. You must be happy about that."

"Yeah, sure."

"I got the impression you liked working there."

"Yeah, it's fine."

"Mr. McCormick tells me you turned down his offer of a job."

He studied his pulpy nails. "Yeah, I'm going to work with my dad."

"Oh? Doing what?"

"He bought a driving range."

Her eyebrows raised. "You're a golfer?"

"No, but he is. And he thinks I'm—I mean *it* is a good investment." He brought his fingers to his mouth and gnawed. In return for working the business, his dad was going to help get him on the poker tournament circuit. It was what he'd dreamed of since he'd played his first video poker game... and being a professional gambler was much more exhilarating than going to medical school.

And more attainable for him, his father had pointed out.

E. gave him a smile. "And do you think you'll like working for your dad?"

"*With* my dad," he corrected. "And sure, who wouldn't want to work with their dad?"

She gave a little laugh. "I wouldn't."

"What does he do?"

"He's in politics. And I'm proud of him, but I wouldn't want to work with him."

"But your dad hasn't been gone most of your life."

"Not in the same sense as your dad," she agreed. "You and your father must be getting along well."

He nodded, then gnawed.

"So you're going to give up the courier job?"

His cover for working collections with Mouse, a henchman for The Carver. "Yeah, that's over."

"And working for the morgue?"

He tasted blood and winced at the zing of pain. "That's over, too."

"I thought you enjoyed working there."

"My dad thinks it's a waste of time."

"And what do you think?"

"I agree. It's not like I'm going to be a doctor or anything." His left leg started to jump.

"So your family is meshing well?" she probed.

"Mostly," he mumbled. "It's going to take a while, I guess, until everything seems normal. My mom is getting better, though."

"That's very good news."

Wes sat forward. "So what will happen when my community service is done?"

"You'll appear before the court and the judge will sign a paper that officially declares your sentence has been served."

"And I won't be coming here anymore?"

She smiled. "Nope, we'll be done."

She seemed more pleased at the prospect than he felt. E. had been a regular part of his life for a long time—he suddenly didn't like the idea of never seeing her again.

"My lawyer is in jail," he reminded her. "And she's batshit crazy. Will that slow things down?"

At the mention of the woman who had been instrumental in her fiancé Leonard's death, E. maintained a stony face. "The court will appoint an attorney to act on your behalf at the proceeding. But you might consider hiring a new attorney to navigate you through the charges lingering from the Vegas incidents."

Anger flared in his chest. "I thought that toady Kelvin Lucas was going to take care of those charges seeing as how he wrongly prosecuted and pursued my dad for a decade?"

"I'm told the D.A.'s office is doing what it can, but the charge of passing counterfeit bills in a casino—not to mention being underage—is serious, Wes. And it's way out of Lucas's jurisdiction. A new attorney would help your cause."

His left knee started to jump. "I'll talk to my dad."

"Okay," she said with a nod, then made a few notes on his file. "That's all for this week."

He wet his lips. "You don't want me to pee in a cup?"

She glanced up from her paperwork. "Your results from last week were clean."

His knee would not stop jumping. "Uh-huh."

She angled her head. "Would you like to leave a sample this week, Wes?"

He swallowed hard. "I think I should."

E. surveyed him with cool green eyes, then opened a drawer and withdrew a bagged cup and lid. "See Officer Scott before you leave."

He reached for the cup, then stood. "Thanks, E." He strode toward the door.

"Wesley?"

He turned back to find her looking concerned.

"Are you going to be okay?"

His sister wasn't really his sister, his girlfriend was halfway around the world, and too soon he'd be spending his days watching grown people hit a little white ball with a metal stick as if it somehow mattered.

"Absolutely." He gave her a little salute, then left.

CHAPTER 3

"Ms. Wren, this is Dr. Denton—the real Dr. Denton, I should add—leaving another voice message. I want to apologize once again for the unfortunate incident last week. Please call me and I'll rearrange my schedule to see you anytime—"

Carlotta deleted the voice message mid-sentence, then shivered over the memory of the encounter. She'd considered calling the police to report the incident, but Dr. Denton was a psychologist with a PhD, not a medical doctor. Impersonating a psychologist was a misdemeanor, at best, and how far would she get pressing charges against a mentally unstable person?

Plus she wasn't keen on revealing she'd spilled her guts to a stranger brandishing a Hello Kitty notebook without questioning his credentials—or his identity. The man could've been a serial killer, for heaven's sake.

Then she sighed. But more likely, he was just another run-of-the-mill Big Fat Liar. A person who enjoyed manipulating others... a person who enjoyed manipulating *her*.

Maybe you're the problem... meaning people saw something in her that put them on the offensive?

She stowed her phone in her bag, then glanced around her girlish bedroom and winced at the cramped clutter and the damaged walls—the bedrooms were next on the renovations list. Dillon Carver's thugs had torn up the townhome looking for counterfeit money Randolph had stashed in a wall. At the time it had felt like a violation, but in hindsight the act had been the impetus to modernize the place.

She was so ready to step out of the past... but it seemed to keep clawing her backward.

Carlotta opened her bedroom door and stepped out into the hallway of the townhome where she'd raised Wes. She glanced at the closed door of his bedroom—she'd heard him leave earlier, but their deal was as long as he kept a python in his room, the door stayed closed. She nursed a pang for shutting him out the past few days, but she wasn't ready to discuss the ramifications of their mother's revelation. Her scant communication had been that he keep everyone—especially Randolph and Valerie—away for the time-being, and she appreciated that he had, at the risk of his own relationship to them.

She turned to stare down the hall to the door of the bedroom her parents had shared when they'd all lived here together. On impulse, she walked to it, compelled to survey the dusty, dated furniture and hastily-left accessories she and Wes had so faithfully preserved. But when she turned the knob, she found it locked. She frowned until a memory surfaced—Wes had mentioned they might use the larger, unused bedroom for storing supplies and tools. Some of the contractors might have insisted he lock up their equipment. Things had been put on hold until...

Until she was able to face the world again?

Or at least face Randolph?

Turning back, she admired the new hardwood in the hallway that led into the living room, which was almost unrecognizable. New drywall, fancy moldings, and fresh paint gave the room a much-needed facelift. The picture window looking onto the front yard had been enlarged and reframed to bathe the room with natural light. She ran a hand over the lustrous leather of the new couch and eyed the complementary armchair... furniture that actually matched, what a novelty. A large wall unit housed a state-of-the-art television and stereo system. Smart, well-placed light fixtures replaced the outdated versions. It was hard to remember how it had all looked before.

Her gaze darted to the corner where a chic floor lamp occupied the spot the tarnished silver Christmas tree had sat for a decade. And lying beneath it all that time had been the momentous secret of her birth. The irony that something she'd preserved for her family had been the undoing of her entire sense of family took her breath away.

The sound of a vehicle pulling into the driveway pulled her out of her thoughts. Her heart buoyed at the sight of Hannah's white van, suddenly bereft she couldn't confide the earth-shaking news to her best friend. But when she had reacted to Valerie's tearful confession by pushing past them to leave, her parents had extracted a promise from her and from Wes not to share the secret with anyone else until they could reconvene and talk about it amongst themselves.

Thankfully Prissy had been off playing with her puppy at the time, so they'd managed to keep it from her, but she was a bright little thing, meaning those days were probably numbered.

She hurried out the door, then jogged down the front steps.

"Carlotta, yoo hoo!"

She winced, then stopped, turned and waved at the woman standing at the fence, holding her dog Toofers. "Hi, Mrs. Winningham." She reached forward to pet Toofers, but yanked her hand back when he snapped at her.

"Have you moved back in?" the woman demanded.

"Yes. My parents are moving to a new home, so I'm back living with Wes."

The woman frowned. "I hope that doesn't mean it's going to get crazy around here again, with hearses and police cars and suspicious-looking characters around at all hours."

"No," Carlotta said, shaking her head. "No suspicious characters."

The van horn sounded, and Hannah Kizer stuck her head out the window. Her black and white striped hair was sculpted into a mohawk and she wore a dog collar. "Ready to roll?"

Mrs. Winningham's mouth tightened into an angry knot. Carlotta yelled, "Coming! Bye, Mrs. Winningham."

She hurried to the van, then opened the door and swung up into the passenger seat. "You saved me."

"What did the old bat want?"

"The usual—letting me know I'm dragging down the neighborhood."

"Yeah, well someone's gotta keep Lindbergh from turning into another Buckhead."

Carlotta laughed. "Thanks for doing this. I gave up the rental car and I need to move the rest of my things back to the townhome before I leave for Dallas."

"No problem." Then Hannah narrowed her eyes. "You look like crap."

"Thanks a lot."

"No, I mean it—you've lost weight, and your skin looks downright green... and that blouse doesn't exactly match those shorts."

Carlotta looked down to see her friend was right. "Uh... I've had the flu," she said, seizing on the excuse she'd given over the phone to consume a few sick days at work.

"Flu season is way the fuck over."

"The stomach flu," she improvised, then busied herself with the seatbelt.

Hannah looked skeptical, then put the van into gear and pulled onto the road into light traffic. "Your mother must be much improved if you moved back in with Wes."

"Yes," Carlotta said, fidgeting. "Plus she and Prissy and Birch will be moving to the new house soon."

"And your dad," Hannah prompted.

"Of course." She glanced out the window to hide her reaction. "Randolph is spending so much time there getting things ready it's as if he's already moved."

"I can't wait to see Miss Priss," Hannah offered.

"Priscilla has a swimming lesson today, and I believe Mom and Randolph are furniture shopping, so it'll be just us." Her father's right-hand man and her mother's caretaker Birch had informed her of their schedule. He seemed aware of the awkward rift in the family, although she wasn't sure if he knew the cause.

"Okay." Then Hannah sighed. "You might as well tell me what's wrong."

Carlotta looked over. "What makes you think something's wrong?"

Hannah pointed to Carlotta's arm. "I can see your nicotine patch. You're in a crisis." Her eyebrows knitted. "Is this about Jack?"

"No."

"Because if he's trying to worm his way back into your bed after what happened with Liz—"

"He isn't," Carlotta broke in. "And I'm not going to let him."

"So you've spoken to him about there being no baby except in that woman's whackadoodle head?"

"No. But I suspect we will at some point."

"Is it Coop then?"

Carlotta sighed. "No. I mean, I know I blew my chance with him. When Rainie told me and Coop about Liz's hysterical pregnancy, I guess I reacted in a way that made Coop think I'd go running back to Jack."

"Kind of convenient for Rainie," Hannah offered dryly, "that she was there to drop the bomb, then be a shoulder for Coop to cry on."

"None of this is Rainie's fault," Carlotta said. "I like her... and I don't blame her for liking Coop. He's a terrific guy."

"Don't I know it," Hannah said with a wistful voice. She'd nursed a crush on Cooper Craft since the first time she'd laid eyes on him.

"How's married life?" Carlotta asked with a laugh.

"For now, the same as single life. We still have our own places. I told Chance I can't introduce him to my parents and we can't live together until he dumps the drug-running business, the escort business, and the porn business."

Carlotta wiped away a smile. "Good for you. What did he say?"

"He says he's going legit, but he hasn't landed on a solid idea yet."

"He could always work for your father," Carlotta offered with a smile.

Hannah's eyes flew wide. "Don't even go there. If Daddy put Chance in charge of one of our hotels, it'd be a brothel in no time."

"By the way, thanks for getting me and Patricia rooms at your family hotel in Dallas. She's beyond giddy to be staying at the Saxler House."

Hannah sniffed. "I still don't understand why you chose that snotface for your assistant."

"She's not that bad," Carlotta murmured. "She has great taste, and she's been a big help planning the new bridal salon."

"She was going to inform on you to the D.A.!'"

"But she didn't."

"Only because you didn't give her any dirt!"

Carlotta made a thoughtful noise. "Patricia's parents lost everything in the Mashburn & Tully Ponzi scheme, and she thought it was Randolph's fault. I can't blame her for being angry." She wet her lips. "Just like I didn't blame you for the same reason."

Hannah's mouth flattened, but if she had more to say, she swallowed it.

At a vibration in her bag, Carlotta reached in to remove her phone.

You have an incoming text from: INMATE PETER ASHFORD at the Fulton County Correctional Facility. To proceed reply YES; to opt out reply NO.

Carlotta made a thoughtful noise.

"Something wrong?"

"It's a text from Peter."

"Richie Rich is texting from jail?" Hannah screeched.

"It's a pilot program, and the texts are monitored."

"Fuck that. Why do they even put people in jail if they get the same privileges as everyone else?"

"Be nice. Peter's not in a good place, physically or mentally."

"Did he send you a dick pic?"

Carlotta rolled her eyes. "Peter wouldn't do that."

"The man's incarcerated. He would *so* do that."

"I just replied that I'll accept the text... I don't know how long it takes before it's actually sent."

"Ten bucks says it's a dick pic."

"I assume the security around communications there is tight."

Hannah scoffed. "Nothing is secure, and men don't care anyway. Do you know how many congressmen have accidentally sent dick pics to every follower they have on social media?"

"I've lost count," Carlotta admitted.

"And every time you think people should know better by now, some other high-profile idiot goes and does it again." She gave Carlotta a pointed look. "So if it's not Jack, or Coop, or Peter who has you down, and your mother is getting better and your career is going gangbusters, then what's wrong?"

Carlotta realized she'd have to toss Hannah a bone. "Maybe it's the reset of everything after being on an adrenaline high for the past several years."

Hannah was silent for so long, Carlotta almost caved and blurted out what was really wrong. Then her friend nodded and said, "That makes sense... and would explain why your immune system is compromised."

She exhaled. "And I'm trying the nicotine patch because with this new position, I can't be stepping out to smoke every time I get the urge."

"Well, good luck with that, although I think you'll need a vice to be able to deal with your new assistant."

Carlotta laughed, relieved to change the subject. They made small talk until they arrived at the Buckhead house where the Wrens had lived prior to Randolph's indictment and subsequent fall from financial and social grace. While he was a fugitive, Randolph had bought back the home under an assumed name. It had been a familiar and comforting environment for Valerie while she struggled to overcome a neurological condition that had stolen her memory. But her mother was getting better every day, and it was time to move on to another home Randolph had purchased to give them a clean start.

And personally, Carlotta would be relieved to see the Buckhead house—another piece of her past—go.

Luckily the house looked quiet, so she hoped they could get in and out quickly. She punched in a code to open the garage door, noting with relief Randolph's car and the SUV Birch drove were both gone. She opened the door to enter the house, and was immediately set upon by a large yellow barking fur ball.

"Hi, Jack," she sputtered between licks and wags. "Did you miss me?"

"Oh, Jesus," Hannah said. "You named the dog Jack?"

"Prissy did," Carlotta said with exasperation, petting the Labrador's head to calm him down. "She was already in love with Jack Terry, and the puppy sealed the deal."

"At least it wasn't a pony."

Carlotta felt wetness on her feet. She looked down to see her striped espadrilles darkened with a telltale stain. The red dye was bleeding like a wound.

"Jack, no!" She cursed, then kicked off her shoes to the tune of Hannah's howling laughter and walked over to open the door to his crate.

"In," she commanded.

Jack sat and looked at her quizzically.

"In," she repeated, pointing. "Go. Now."

He laid down and put his paws over his nose.

"Oooh!" She backtracked and found a paper towel to clean up the mess, then tossed her cloth shoes in the trash. Then she glanced at her watch. "Come on, Hannah. We don't have much time." She walked to the stairs and took them two at a time. Jack was on their heels.

Hannah frowned. "Why?"

"I, uh… want to get packed up and leave before everyone gets home. I don't want a scene."

"Why would there be a scene?"

Heat flooded her face. "Things have been a little tense, that's all. Too much togetherness, I suppose."

"Okay," Hannah said, her voice questioning. "I didn't realize this was a covert operation."

"Let's just do this as quickly as possible." She padded down the hallway to her childhood bedroom. Jack loped along beside her, panting like a man.

When Carlotta opened the door, she winced at the disarray. Clothes were strewn from corner to corner, books and papers covered the bed, and toiletries spilled out of the bathroom.

"Did you leave in a hurry?" Hannah asked, picking up a spilled can of soda. The sticky pool of liquid had congealed.

"I guess so," Carlotta murmured, thinking back to the moment her mother's pronouncement about the photo in the locket had sunk in.

Carlotta… he's your real father.

At that awful moment, she couldn't even look at them—all she could think of was getting out of there. She'd shaken off her parents' attempts to talk to her, had run blindly up the stairs to get her purse and call an Uber. In a haze, she'd torn through her room for essentials and had stuffed a few clothes into a duffel bag.

"Yikes," Hannah said, circling in place. "It looks like a bomb went off in here."

24

Which was how her heart had felt that night. Giving herself a mental shake, she opened her tote to remove a box of garbage bags. After ripping it open, she handed a plastic bag to Hannah. "Everything goes, you don't have to be gentle."

"It's going to be one hell of a mess to unpack."

"Probably," Carlotta admitted. She pushed her feet into a pair of sandals sticking out from under a chair, then began to stuff a bag full of whatever she put her hands on. They established a routine—she'd fill a bag and Hannah carried it to the van, and by the time she returned to the bedroom, Carlotta had another bag ready to go. Jack ran back and forth barking and lunging at them and generally being a pain in the ass, not unlike his namesake, Carlotta noted. She didn't stop to process anything, just shoved it all in to deal with later. Gradually, the room emptied. She worked up a sweat and Hannah's boots were falling heavier on the steps when the last bag was cinched tight.

"It's a good thing this is it," Hannah said with a huff. "The van is stuffed full. You might have to ride home on the hood."

Carlotta smiled, then turned to scan her old bedroom one last time. She would probably never set foot in it again. "Goodbye, old friend."

"Are you going to fucking cry?" Hannah asked.

"No," Carlotta said with a sigh. "Let's go."

As they walked down the stairs a chime sounded, indicating a door on the first floor had opened. Jack was instantly alert, and ran downstairs barking. Carlotta heard Prissy's high-pitched voice and winced, hoping only her sister and Birch had arrived, but when she and Hannah walked into the kitchen, Prissy was petting Jack, Birch was carrying a bag of groceries, and her parents were bringing up the rear.

Correction—her mother and the man she *thought* was her father. She made eye contact with Randolph and Valerie, and they both looked pained.

"Carlotta!" Prissy shouted, and ran to hug her. Carlotta's heart welled with love for the little girl—she was a precocious kid, but she was the glue that had held them all together during this shaky period of getting to know each other again.

"Where have you been?" Prissy demanded. "You left the night we opened Christmas gifts and didn't say goodbye."

"I haven't been feeling well," Carlotta said—not a lie. "I'm sorry I had to leave so suddenly."

"Are you coming back here to live?" the girl asked. She was a mirror image of herself at the same age.

Carlotta shook her head. "No. I'm going back to live with Wesley. And you'll be moving to the new house soon—are you excited about your new room? And a pool?"

"I guess so," girl said, working her mouth back and forth. "It's why I'm taking swimming classes."

"And how's that going?" Hannah asked.

Prissy made a face. "The chlorine isn't good for my hair."

They all laughed, and it helped to break the tension in the air.

"I need for you to take me shopping," Prissy said to Carlotta.

"I'm leaving for Dallas tomorrow for business. I'll be away for a week... can it wait till I return?"

Prissy nodded. "I need a dress and sandals... and a new bathing suit. And probably a hat."

Carlotta saluted. "And by the time I get back, you'll be moved into the new house." She glanced to her mother. "I removed everything from my old room."

Valerie gave her a sad smile and nodded. "So you're feeling... better?"

"Some," Carlotta said. "But not completely."

"Do you have time to... talk about it?" Valerie asked.

"No." Carlotta said, signaling Hannah. "We were just leaving."

"But you'll call sometime... soon?" Randolph asked.

"When I get back in town," Carlotta said vaguely, then walked to them and gave them each a quick hug. Randolph was stiff, but so was she.

"We love you," her mother whispered, and hung on a few seconds longer.

Carlotta didn't trust herself to respond—she didn't want to say anything to tip off Hannah or Prissy. She said goodbye to Birch, who seemed to be studying them curiously. So he didn't know—a fact that struck her as odd since he seemed to be Randolph's primary confidante.

The house suddenly seemed stifling, and she felt a huge sense of relief to be leaving. Prissy and Jack the puppy followed them outside.

"Look how much he's grown," Prissy said, rubbing his ears.

"His bladder hasn't grown," Carlotta said wryly.

"Where has Mr. Jack the policeman been?"

"Busy. But I'm sure he'll come see you sometime."

She gave Prissy a goodbye hug, then climbed back into the stuffed van.

"That was a little weird with your folks," Hannah commented as she backed the van out onto the street.

"I didn't notice," Carlotta murmured. Her phone dinged and she pulled it from her purse. "It's the text from Peter... oh."

"What is it?" Hannah asked.

Carlotta eyes went wide. "I owe you ten dollars."

"Toldja!" Hannah crowed. "Let me see!"

"No! Besides... it doesn't look like... him."

"Oh, so you've actually seen it?"

Carlotta rolled her eyes. "You know I have."

"And how does he compare to Jack?"

Carlotta scoffed. "I'm not going to answer that."

"Oh, come on—they're both out of your life, or so you say."

"Still. They're too different to compare."

"We're not talking a lot of variables here—who's hung better? And while we're at it, let's throw Coop in the lineup."

"*Stop.*"

"So you're saying you have slept with Coop?"

"No, I'm not saying that."

"Ah, so you haven't."

"Enough, Hannah!"

Her phone dinged and she looked down. "Here's another one. That's *definitely* not him."

Hannah craned for a look. "Damn. Too bad. But why is Peter sending you dick pics of someone else's dick?"

"It's obviously some kind of mistake."

"Send them to me, I'm going to start a pornographic Pinterest board on the Dark Web."

Carlotta laughed. "I haven't heard you talk about culinary school for a while."

"I know... I need to finish. My dad is leaning on me to get more involved in the property business. I guess I'm putting off my career decision." Then she smirked. "But *you* don't have that problem, Miss Director. When you get back from Dallas, let's do something to celebrate your promotion. You're killing it, girl."

Carlotta smiled. Leave it to Hannah to cheer her up. She settled back in the seat and sighed. "Yeah... I am kind of killing it, aren't I?"

CHAPTER 4

PLEASE BE advised the Fulton County Correctional System pilot texting program has been terminated due to a hacking incident. If you received a lewd image, please accept our deepest apologies and delete the image from your device. If you need assistance, take your device to any Atlanta Police Dept building or ask any APD officer to help you.

Sitting on a southbound train, one hand on her swaying suitcase, Carlotta shook her head. That explained the bizarre erotic photos she'd received that kept reappearing every time she deleted them. She made a mental note to visit Peter in person when she returned from Dallas. She wanted to make sure he was as good as one could be while incarcerated, and to find out the latest on his case. And something he'd said in a phone call to her about Randolph kept playing over in her mind.

He's not... what you think he is.

Did he know Randolph wasn't her real father? Had he been trying to forewarn her?

And did he know the identity of her real father?

She idly stroked the locket pendant. Her phone vibrated again and she braced herself for another unwanted text image. Instead, Coop's name popped up with a message.

Have u blocked me? Just saying hi and I hope u are well.

She smiled, then texted back, *Haven't blocked u, just swamped.*

Phew, was starting to feel like a stalker.

I've had stalkers and you're not one. Sorry to be MIA... have been wanting to talk to u.

Sure... meet u at Moody's sometime soon?

29

On the train, heading to Dallas for business. Ping u when I get back?

Sure thing. Stay out of trouble.

Her heart swelled and she wished like hell she could hit the rewind button. When Rainie had dropped the bombshell that Liz wasn't expecting Jack's baby, she should've shrugged it off and gone home with Coop like she'd planned. Instead she'd run to the bathroom to collect herself like a teenager at the prom. She didn't blame Coop for giving up on her. Her own heart had whiplash from bouncing between the three men in her life.

She wanted her next step in that department to be more stabilizing... and long-term. But she couldn't even think about that until she worked through this latest twist in the Wren family drama.

In need of a good distraction, she reached into her tote and pulled out the promotion gift to herself—a sterling silver business card holder, customized with her initials in lead glass crystals. She opened it and slid out a crisp white card.

Carlotta Wren, Director, Atlanta Bridal Salon

With the inimitable flourish of the Neiman Marcus name at the bottom, of course.

She ran her finger over the raised letters, reveling. It was fulfilling to be acknowledged for doing something well, in an industry she loved. To date, the build-out of the bridal salon was going well, and feature designers had been chosen. The merchandise would start to arrive soon, with a grand opening planned in a mere three months. This week in Dallas would be spent with the director of the infamous flagship salon, learning the ins and outs of the specialty business.

In truth, she was nervous. Lindy had paid her a huge compliment by offering the job in spite of her somewhat checkered employee record, so a lot was riding on her performance.

When the conductor announced the airport station, she closed the card holder and pushed it back into her purse. A sharp pain stabbed her hand—she yanked it out to find a drop of blood on her thumb, then realized a prong around one of the crystals was sticking up. But it would have to wait.

Sucking her throbbing thumb, she managed to emerge from the train with a compact rolling suitcase and tote bag, and head to the lower level lobby. After passing through the turnstiles, she walked with a herd of passengers out of the train terminal and into the teeming Atlanta Hartsfield-Jackson International Airport. She considered checking the roll-on, but the bag check line at the airline ticketing counter was ominously long and since she was already pressed for time, she skipped it and made her way to the security line that was moving alarmingly slow.

But surrounded by lots of smartly-dressed professionals, she gave in to a happy feeling of unexpected pride. She was traveling on a bona fide business trip, like a normal young woman with a promising career—it seemed alien... but good. She received a couple of admiring glances in her olive-colored Veronica Beard skirt and floral blouse. She'd added a lavender Johnny Was scarf in case the plane was chilly.

She felt put-together and cosmopolitan... and glad she had something of substance in her life to take her mind off the low hum of grief running through her veins. Finding out Randolph wasn't her real father was like finding out the earth was square. Her entire belief system was teetering—everything seemed up for grabs.

As the security line inched along, her mind wandered. In hindsight, her memory-impaired mother had been dropping little hints, all along, like the day they'd all been having breakfast and Prissy had asked her why she called their daddy "Randolph"?

I guess I'm still getting used to having him around.

But your father isn't here, Valerie had insisted.

And the day they'd spent in Piedmont Park.

Your father and I came here all the time... when he was still in love with me.

Dad is still in love with you, Mom.

Valerie had shaken her head. *Your dad isn't around.*

At the time she had dismissed the awkward remarks, thinking her mother was remembering a time when Randolph wasn't there for her emotionally. But now she realized Valerie could've been thinking about another man—her biological father.

"Shoes, belts and liquids in a bin, bags flat," a TSA security guard called.

Carlotta complied, putting the taupe Chloe pumps into a bin with an apologetic twinge. They deserved more respect.

The red-haired woman in front of her turned back. "This is more clothes than I took off for my date last night."

Carlotta laughed in solidarity, then waited until the woman walked through the scanner before padding forward to do the same. She assumed the "jumping jack" position, wondering just how many anatomical details were discernible. When she was waved through, she waited for her bins, happy to be reunited with her lovely shoes.

Two lines over, though, a small commotion had erupted.

"Someone took my phone!" a familiar voice cried.

Carlotta craned her neck to see Patricia Alexander dead center, sending glares all around. The blond woman's taste could best be described as Sorority Girl Chic—lots of pink and green, lots of hairspray. Some people lifted their hands in denial and began to back away.

Carlotta threaded her way through the crowd. "Patricia, hi. Is everything okay?"

Patricia turned her head, but her flash of friendly recognition was brief. "No, everything is *not* okay. My phone was in my purse before I sent it through the scanner, and now it isn't." She shot an accusatory glance toward the nearest TSA agent, a guy with a deadpan expression.

"Ma'am, are you sure it isn't in your purse?" he asked in a tired monotone.

"I looked, and it's not in here." She lifted the white Longchamp shoulder tote and gave it a shake for emphasis.

"How about your other bag?" he asked, pointing to the large black makeup case she held in the opposite hand.

"My phone was in my purse," she insisted through clenched teeth.

He gave her an indulgent little smile. "Okay. Why don't we step over here and take another look?"

Patricia's body language was stiff, but she followed the man to a nearby station. Carlotta hovered nearby in case Patricia needed her, but glanced at her watch. Their flight would begin boarding in a few minutes, and getting from concourse to concourse in the sprawling airport required a little time.

"Take your time, ma'am," the agent said. "You can remove items and place them here on the table if you want to."

"I'll hold your makeup case," Carlotta offered.

Patricia handed it to her with an eyeroll over the situation, then turned back to remove things from her bag with jerky motions. Onto the table went a Tory Burch wallet, a pair of Dolce & Gabbana sunglasses, an inflatable neck pillow, an eye mask, a pair of sleep socks, a copy of *Bride* magazine, a copy of *Gun & Garden* magazine, a copy of *Modern Cat* magazine, a copy of *Dating* magazine, a pad of pink legal paper, several pens and markers, a set of earbuds, a business card holder, and… Patricia's hand stilled, then she removed a phone.

The man gave her a flat smile. "Is that the phone you were looking for, ma'am?"

"Yes," she squeaked, then touched her forehead. "I don't know how I missed it."

"Uh-huh."

"Easy mistake," Carlotta said. "We should get going if we're going to make our flight."

"Okay," Patricia snapped, tossing things back into her purse with more fervor than necessary. "I'm hurrying."

Carlotta bit her tongue, but let the comment pass in the essence of time. "Thank you," she mouthed to the TSA agent.

"I saw that," Patricia said. "You don't have to thank him for doing his job."

Carlotta swallowed hard. They had to get through an entire week together. "Are you ready?"

"Yes," Patricia said, then gave the agent a haughty look and flounced away.

Carlotta handed her the makeup case. "Are you okay? You seem on edge."

Patricia's brow furrowed. "I don't like to fly… everything about travel is so stressful."

"Only if you let it be." Carlotta stepped into the stream of people heading toward the shuttle that traveled between concourses. "I thought you were looking forward to this trip."

"Oh, I am. Don't worry, boss—I popped a Xanax. It'll kick in before we get on the plane."

"You don't have to call me boss," Carlotta murmured, wondering if the tranquilizer had already started to "kick in."

"I don't mind," Patricia chirped, then stumbled, nearly taking out the guy walking in front of her. "Sorry," she called. Then she puffed out her cheeks. "I just want to get there already."

Carlotta tamped down a spike of frustration. She flashed back to Hannah's prediction that working with Patricia would have her smoking again, but reminded herself not everyone traveled well and the woman would probably be more like herself when they landed.

Otherwise, this was going to be a long week.

"You're traveling light," Carlotta said, nodding to the makeup case. "I assume you checked a bag?"

"Two of them. We'll be there for an entire week—didn't you?"

"I was able to pack enough in my roll-on," she murmured. Not true. But with most of her clothes still in garbage bags, she hadn't had much to choose from. She might have to shop for a few things, if the schedule allowed.

But first, they had to make their flight.

The shuttle lines were long and it took more time than they expected to get to their concourse. They wound up jogging to their gate, which was deserted except for a vested agent whose head was on a pivot. "Wren and Alexander?"

"That's us," Carlotta called.

She scanned their boarding passes and waved them through the door. "You just made it."

"Ugh, I hate to board late," Patricia groused as they hurried down the jetway. "There's never enough room in the overhead bins."

"Let's just be thankful we didn't miss our flight," Carlotta chided.

A flight attendant met them with a smile. "Please get settled as quickly as possible. We're ready to take off."

Carlotta avoided eye contact with glaring passengers, although she received a sympathetic look from the red-haired woman she'd laughed with in the security line. She and Patricia scrambled to find a spot in the overheads for her roll-on bag and for Patricia's makeup case, then fell into their window and middle seats after their irritated rowmate, a stoic-faced matron, stood to let them in.

"Can I have the window seat?" Patricia asked.

Carlotta gave her a flat smile, then nodded and they played musical chairs again to the sounds of groans all around. She settled into the center seat, squeezed between the sour-faced woman and Patricia, who, despite her slender build, seemed to occupy every inch of her seat and more.

At that moment, Carlotta would've given a kidney for a cigarette. Unfiltered. Instead she massaged the nicotine patch on the back of her arm through her blouse, and popped a piece of chewing gum.

The safety demonstration was mercifully quick. And the plane must've been first in line for takeoff because seconds later, they were taxiing, then in the air. She glanced over to see Patricia clasping the armrests with a white-knuckled grip, her eyes closed. Carlotta was shot through with gratitude she wasn't besieged with crippling anxiety like some people, and vowed to be more tolerant of the woman.

If there was an upside to her parents' absence, she supposed it was the resilience she'd been forced to cultivate. In the wake of her mother's recent admission, she had the answer to a question that had always eaten at her: How could her father abandon his own daughter and leave her with so much to contend with? He'd said it was to spare her from even more danger and responsibility if he and Valerie had stayed, or if they'd come back, but now she knew:

He'd been able to leave her because she wasn't his daughter.

And the knowledge hurt—deeply.

Next to her, Patricia opened one eye, then the other, and heaved a sigh. "At least our seats are together so we can chat."

Carlotta nodded. "I'd like to go over some things before the meeting tomorrow morning."

Patricia's face fell. "Oh."

"Or maybe we could do it over dinner this evening?"

Patricia winced. "I have a confession to make. I have a date with a guy I met online."

Carlotta raised an eyebrow.

"I won't let it interfere with work this week," she added quickly, then looked contrite. "I guess the thought of meeting John face to face is amping up my anxiety."

"If you're that worried, maybe you shouldn't meet him," Carlotta offered lightly.

"But what if he's the one? Wouldn't it make a great story to tell our kids?"

"I suppose so. You must know this guy pretty well if you're already thinking about kids."

She nodded. "We both swiped right two weeks ago today."

Carlotta tried to maintain her smile. "That sounds... fast."

"Not really." Patricia patted the copy of *Dating* magazine in her lap. "Some people go on two dates every day, and three on Saturday."

"That doesn't mean it's best... or safe, for that matter."

Patricia frowned. "You don't have to rain on my parade, Carlotta, just because you're still single."

Carlotta frowned back. "I'm just saying be careful. There are a lot of crazy people out there." Like the patient of Dr. Denton's who'd extracted her life story. "You shouldn't be so trusting."

"Maybe *you* shouldn't be so suspicious," Patricia shot back. "John is a terrific guy."

"John? Is his last name Smith?"

Patricia pursed her mouth. "As a matter of fact, it is, but he spells with a 'y' instead of an 'i' and there's an 'e' on the end, so it's not made up."

Carlotta pushed her tongue into her cheek. "Patricia, please don't meet this guy. He's probably lying about who he is."

"How would you know?"

"Because that's what people *do*," Carlotta said with rising ire. "They lie every day, all the time, every chance they get!"

Patricia sputtered. "If this is about me taking the job at Neiman's to inform on you to the D.A.'s office, I said I was sorry!"

"Excuse me."

Carlotta turned her head to see a flight attendant leaning in.

"Is there a problem here?" he asked.

She hadn't realized their voices had carried. "Um, no," she replied, feeling foolish. "No problem."

"She's my boss," Patricia supplied helpfully.

"They're arguing over a man," their rowmate added with an eyeroll.

"That's not true," Carlotta said quickly.

"Well, it's kind of true," Patricia said.

The flight attendant looked back and forth. "Perhaps one of you would like to change seats?"

"That won't be necessary," Carlotta said, waving her hand.

"Because I'm going to sleep," Patricia said matter-of-factly, as if the incident were all Carlotta's fault. Then she pulled her sleep mask, ear plugs, and neck pillow out of her purse, and proceeded to blow noisily into the cushion to inflate it.

"I apologize for the disturbance," Carlotta murmured to the attendant. "It won't happen again."

"Good," he said with a pointed look, then walked away.

Feeling utterly chastised, Carlotta shrank into the seat. Patricia ignored her, donned her sleep accessories, and within five minutes, was snoring like a man. When her *Dating* magazine slid off her lap, Carlotta caught it. Then with nothing else to do, she began to idly flip through the pages.

"How to Set up an Irresistible Online Profile"... "Shoot a Sexy Selfie"... "When Should You Disclose Your STD?" She read each article with part fascination, part dismay at what lengths men and women were willing to go to in order to find a partner— including lie. Worse—people admitted they sometimes lied to make themselves sound better, and they expected the people they met also to be lying to a certain degree. Veteran online daters even had clever names for the practice: "embellishing," "enhancing," and the more-audacious "personal branding."

Ugh.

When the same flight attendant came by with a snack cart and leveled his gaze on her, Carlotta demurred and went back to her magazine. But she didn't see anything in the publication that made any kind of dating sound appealing. By the time the captain announced they were starting their initial descent into Dallas, she was beyond ready to be off the plane and stretch her legs.

And remain single.

She shook Patricia's shoulder to rouse her from her sleep. "We're getting ready to land."

Patricia slowly came around and dismantled her setup, nursing a frown. "Ugh, I have a headache from the Xanax. I might have to pass on meeting John for dinner after all."

Carlotta pressed her lips together. "I have aspirin."

"No, thanks. I don't like to mix meds." Patricia looked contrite as she straightened her clothes. "I'm sorry if I was cranky before. And I was rude to the TSA guy—the truth is I lose my phone all the time. The Xanax does that to me sometimes."

"Then why take it?"

"Because being an absent-minded bitch is better than being scared."

Her voice was hard, but her expression was vulnerable. Sympathy barbed through Carlotta's chest. Patricia had issues... but then, who didn't?

The airplane touched down hard, jarring them, then taxied to a stop.

"Ladies and gentlemen," came the announcement over the P.A., "welcome to Dallas, Texas. It is now safe to use cell phones and wireless devices. Thank you for flying with us."

Carlotta reached into her bag and turned on her cell phone. It immediately lit up with incoming texts—almost all of them pornographic images of penises that appeared to be on some kind of loop.

And a text from Hannah.

Scored you and Barbie upgraded rooms at the hotel. Cheers.

Carlotta smiled, then texted *Thanks*

No problem. How's that going, btw?

You can say I told you so.

Ha! Well, if you're gonna off her, do it in Texas. They'll understand.

Carlotta smothered a laugh. *Later.*

"Barbie?" Patricia said.

Carlotta turned her head and realized with mortification Patricia had seen the text messages.

"That's what you and your Goth friend call me—Barbie?"

"Hannah is trying to be funny. She doesn't mean anything by it."

"And what did you mean by she could say 'I told you so'?"

Carlotta wet her lips. "Nothing. It was a bad joke. I apologize."

Patricia's eyes went cold. "Did you give me this job to get revenge for what I did? So you could order me around and make fun of me behind my back?"

"What? No, of course not. I gave you this job because I thought you would be good at it. But you can be a bit of a pill sometimes, Patricia."

"So can you," the blonde flung back. "You sashay around Neiman's like you own the place, come and go when you want and play Nancy Drew in between."

Carlotta's mouth tightened. "I put in more hours than I turn in. And I'm good at my job."

"Everyone who works there knows you used to buy high-end merchandise on your employee discount, wear it, then return it all for full credit."

"That was wrong," Carlotta admitted. "And that was a long time ago. I paid the store back."

"That's the point," Patricia said, her eyes flashing. "You should've been fired—anyone else would've been. Lindy keeps looking the other way because she feels sorry for you, poor little Carlotta whose parents abandoned her. Well, boo freaking *hoo!*"

Carlotta realized the air around them had grown dead quiet. She turned to see their rowmate and other passengers staring at them. The flight attendant from earlier trotted down the aisle.

"Seriously, what is the problem here?" he demanded.

Carlotta lifted her hand. "I'm sorry. It's just a misunderstanding between friends."

"We're not friends," Patricia said defiantly.

"Coworkers," Carlotta corrected calmly. "Sorry for the disturbance. Everything is fine."

The flight attendant crossed his arms. "For the safety of everyone else, I think it would be best if you both deplane first."

Carlotta pressed her lips together, then nodded. She gathered her tote bag and stood to sidle past their rowmate and the attendant. She glanced back to see Patricia was following more slowly and with angry body language. Carlotta's skin sizzled with embarrassment as she opened three overhead bins to find her roll-on bag, heave it down, then walked past hundreds of reproachful eyes. Her mind raced with recrimination. Her first position as a manager, and she'd already made a huge misstep with her only subordinate.

Worse—she actually thought she and Patricia would make a good team to launch the Neiman's bridal salon in Atlanta and attempt to replicate the success of the flagship salon in Dallas.

As she exited the plane she offered an apologetic smile to the other flight attendants. In the jetway she slowed her pace to wait for Patricia. The woman exited a few seconds later with her purse and makeup case in-hand. She wouldn't make eye contact.

Carlotta inhaled, then fell in step beside her. "Patricia, I'm sorry. I was wrong, and I hope you can forgive me. I really do want to work with you."

The woman's mouth tightened. "I can't think right now. I have a headache."

Carlotta nodded. "Fair enough. We can talk later. Let's get your bags and head to the hotel."

They strode to baggage claim wordlessly. Carlotta's stomach churned. Maybe she wasn't cut out for being a manager. Maybe she wasn't meant to be anything more than a sales associate—it was an honorable job and she excelled at it. Maybe she should call Lindy and tell her to find someone else to open the salon, before she cratered the entire project.

"My bags are already here," Patricia said, pointing to the carousel.

One advantage to almost missing the plane, Carlotta thought wryly. The bags had probably been added to the cargo hold last.

Patricia handed her purse and makeup case to Carlotta and proceeded to wrestle the luggage onto a rolling cart. Carlotta glanced around, relieved they'd be out of baggage claim before all the irritated passengers from their flight showed up. Together they rolled the cart through automatic doors to the outside.

Carlotta blinked and broke into an instant sweat. Dallas, Texas was sunny and *hot*... not a damp, sticky hot like Atlanta hot, but a sizzling, meat-on-a-grill hot.

"Ugh," Patricia said. "If things go well with John, he will have to move to Georgia."

Carlotta decided to keep her thoughts on 'John' to herself this time. They walked a few feet to a taxi kiosk and gave the man working it the name of their hotel.

"Nice place," he offered, signaling a cabbie and making a note on a log. He was slicked-back handsome and spoke with a smooth drawl. "What are you ladies in town for?" He smiled at Patricia's legs.

"We work for Neiman Marcus," Patricia offered.

"Another nice place." He flexed his beefy shoulders. "I could use a new suit."

Patricia withdrew her business card holder, then flicked out a card and extended it. "So call me while I'm in town."

He took the card, then read it and balked good-naturedly. "Bridal salon? Sorry, I'm not looking to get married."

Patricia winked. "Neither am I."

A lie, Carlotta noted with amusement. Patricia was on a constant hunt for a husband, and her recent failed engagement seemed to have fueled her fervor. But what man would go out with a woman who stated her matrimonial intents up front?

So maybe the article she'd read on the plane was correct in asserting that when it came to relationships, some lying was helpful in the long run.

A taxi pulled up and Carlotta slid inside, surreptitiously watching the interplay between Patricia and the man. He gave her a big, charming smile. She gave him a big tip. He helped her into the car, took one last look at her legs, then closed the door.

Patricia gave him a little wave as they pulled away. "So far, I like Texan men."

Carlotta was grateful to be back on neutral speaking terms. "I do hope your online friend John turns out to be as great as you think he is."

"Thanks," Patricia chirped. Then she pulled out her phone and turned her shoulder to indicate things still weren't good between them.

Minus ten.

CHAPTER 5

THINKING IT best to let Patricia stew—and to allow the anxiety medication to fully wear off—Carlotta took in the skyline of Dallas and tried to get a feel for the place from the passing scenery. The city was more compact than Atlanta, the buildings and activity more concentrated. But she liked it. Funny, she'd never considered living anywhere other than Atlanta. Peter had once asked her to move to New York City with him, but the timing had been wrong. Now she wondered where her life—and his—would be if she'd accepted. Looking back, he'd probably been worried even then about being embroiled in something underhanded at Mashburn & Tully, even if he wasn't sure what was going on.

She was looking forward to spending time in a different city. There was a big world outside of Atlanta, Georgia, and now she had fewer ties to keep her there. Wes was a young man and working for Randolph, who would keep him on the straight and narrow better than she could. And she had no one special keeping her rooted there.

Her phone vibrated with a text. She expected to see more penises flying at her. Instead it was a text from Jack.

Are u ghosting me?

She smiled, then texted *Since when do u know what ghosting means?*

Hey I'm hip.

Not if u use the word hip.

Ouch. Just checking in to see if you're still alive.

She bit into her lip. Was he fishing? Was he checking to see if she were alive… or alive and available? *I'm still alive.*

Good. Stay that way. See you sometime.

Carlotta shook her head at her own folly for thinking she'd ever get a clear message from Jack Terry. She stowed her phone just as the cabbie announced they were arriving at the Saxler House.

The hotel was a showpiece, to be sure. Standing twelve stories high, the curving black building looked more like a piece of sleek sculpture than a place of business. The only relief to its modernity were enormous trees and giant flowering bushes around its soaring entrance. Carlotta exhaled in appreciation.

Despite Patricia's mood, she seemed equally transfixed. "Wow. Your Goth friend's family owns this place?"

"Yes."

"Life just isn't fair," Patricia murmured, then opened the door to climb out.

Carlotta paid the fare and tip, then followed. A steward appeared to greet them and take care of their luggage. They walked inside the hotel and were immediately transported. The lobby was grand in scale, furnished with oversized pieces of art and furniture. In a corner a jazz trio provided soothing background music. The reception desk was made of satiny burled wood and followed the curve of the building. Each member of the staff looked as if they were dressed for a cocktail party.

They were greeted warmly, and the associate's eyes lit up when she pulled up their reservation. "You have two of our penthouse suites." She pushed electronic keys the size of flash drives across the counter. "And if you like, you can download the hotel app and access your room through a mobile device."

"I've already done it," Patricia said, holding up her phone.

"I'm not very techy," Carlotta said.

"If only you had an assistant to show you," Patricia said lightly.

Carlotta recognized an olive branch when she saw one. "Will you help me?"

"Of course." She took Carlotta's phone and by the time the clerk had processed the room payment, Patricia handed it back. "Done. All you need to do is set up a four-digit code to unlock the door, like this."

She demonstrated on her phone, and Carlotta followed along. "Okay, got it... I think."

"Enjoy your stay," the desk clerk said, "and let us know if we can be of service."

Carlotta and Patricia followed the luggage steward to the elevator, who pointed to a service elevator and indicated he would meet them at their rooms. Everywhere they looked, opulence exuded. Every surface sparkled, every décor accessory was perfection.

"Again, life isn't fair," Patricia said with a little frown.

"It can seem that way," Carlotta agreed. "But it all evens out in the end."

"You think?"

"I hope," Carlotta added. "Besides, think of the people who will never get to stay in a place like this."

"You're right," Patricia murmured as they walked onto the glossy elevator.

Carlotta wet her lips. "So... are we okay?"

Patricia was quiet, then sighed. "Sure. I behaved badly, you behaved badly... like you said, I guess it all evens out."

"Good," Carlotta said with relief. "And thank you, Patricia. I can't pull off this project without you."

"I'm not sure about that, Carlotta. I think you could do whatever you set your mind to."

At the unexpected compliment, her lips parted. "That's kind of you to say, and I'm sure I don't deserve it."

Patricia shrugged. "I call it the way I see it."

The elevator doors opened and she walked out. Carlotta followed, nonplused.

Their rooms were across the hall from each other.

"Let's see if our apps work," Patricia said, then tapped in her code. A light on the lock flashed green. "Mine works."

Carlotta tried hers, and smiled when the lock on her door flashed green. "Mine, too." She turned the handle and opened the door... into a sanctuary.

"Oh, my," Carlotta uttered.

"Wow," Patricia said, indicating her room was equally impressive.

One long wall was a solid sheet of glass. Despite the late afternoon sunshine pouring in, the room was cool and shady. A black hardwood floor led to a low bed covered with white linen sheets. Over the bed, an enormous paddle fan turned leisurely. To the left was a bathroom with a waterfall shower. To the right was a sitting room with a spacious desk and work area. Top-of-the-line electronics were suspended on strategic walls.

She could tolerate a week in this place.

"Not bad," Patricia said from the hallway. "Tell your friend I said thanks for the upgrade."

Carlotta nodded. "I will. "

The porter arrived with their luggage. He unloaded Carlotta's roll-on bag and wheeled it into her room, hoisting it onto a luggage valet for her to open and unpack. She tipped him. Patricia picked up her black cosmetic case, but let the man wrangle her larger bags.

"So what time should we leave in the morning?" Patricia asked.

"Our meeting is at nine, and the store is within walking distance, so how about eight-thirty, in the lobby? And remember we're on Central time."

"Okay." Then Patricia stepped forward and peered at the locket Carlotta wore. "That's a pretty piece of jewelry. I haven't seen you wear it before."

"It's a family heirloom," Carlotta said, reaching up to clasp the pendant between finger and thumb.

"Is there a picture of someone special inside?"

Still pinging with regret from the texting snafu, Carlotta felt compelled to share something with the woman. What harm would it do? She opened the locket and revealed the tiny black and white photo. "He's a distant relative, but I don't know his name."

"Hm... he looks familiar."

Carlotta's heart skipped a beat. "Really? You know this man?"

Patricia squinted. "Maybe... I don't know. I have a thing for faces." Then she shook her head. "But I don't think so—and that would be weird anyway, right, if I knew your relative? It's a pretty necklace, though."

"Thanks," Carlotta said, struggling to get her vitals under control. "Have fun at dinner."

Patricia started to turn away, then looked back with a guilty expression. "What are you going to do this evening?"

"I have some reports to go over and emails to send. And I'll get a bite to eat somewhere."

"Okay, then. I'll see you in the morning, in the lobby."

Carlotta nodded, then closed the door as Patricia was tipping the porter. She heaved an exhale, then stepped out of her shoes and padded to the bathroom to wash her face. When she leaned over the sink, the locket fell forward. She unfastened it and studied the picture for the hundredth time. The man had dark hair, although with a black and white picture, it could be almost any color. He wasn't smiling, or frowning. And he wasn't looking directly at the camera, so it was impossible to tell anything about his eyes. She couldn't tell anything about him at all, really, whether he was happy, or depressed... a good person, or depraved.

And she didn't know if she wanted to know.

She set down the locket, then turned on the cold water and splashed her face several times in an attempt to wash away the troubling thoughts that were never more than a heartbeat away. Then she toweled off, pulled the tail of her blouse from her skirt, and began to unpack. By the time the suitcase was empty, she was seriously regretting her hasty clothing choices, but it would have to do.

From her tote she removed the small laptop she'd been given to help manage the salon buildout. She'd been thrown headfirst into the world of business emails—thank God for spellcheckers—and endless spreadsheets. At first it was overwhelming, but Birch had been a dear to teach her some basics, and on a couple of occasions, Prissy had shown her how to do some things. The kid looked like her, but she had Wesley's smarts.

Carlotta bit down on her tongue—Wesley and Prissy both had Randolph's smarts... because they were his children.

She stopped the careening train of thought and opened the laptop to focus on business correspondence. Among the messages was a note from the manager of the Dallas bridal salon saying how much she was looking forward to meeting Carlotta, and how many good things Lindy had to say about her.

An embellishment on Lindy's part, Carlotta thought wryly. But she was going to do everything she could to prove Lindy right, to make this trip productive, and leave with a good handle on how to make the new bridal salon a success.

The next time she looked up, the sun was beginning to set. She stood and stretched her tired shoulders, and her stomach growled.

She considered venturing out for dinner, but she was also looking forward to going to bed early. Last night she'd gotten next to no sleep worrying about the trip and last-minute details, and she wanted to be fresh for tomorrow's meetings which would likely last all day. Yet she didn't want to order room service. Settling on the hotel restaurant, she repaired her makeup and her outfit, then picked up her tote and left the room.

Across the hall, Patricia's room was quiet, so she'd probably already left to meet her online date. Carlotta threw up a prayer the man wasn't a serial killer, then made her way down to the restaurant.

The place was crowded—not surprising for the caliber of the hotel—so she opted to eat at the bar. She found an empty stool and swiveled to take in all the décor, including the people, who were as beautiful as their luxe surroundings. It was a sexy room of black and steel and red velvet, with flattering lighting and just the right acoustics for a cozy clatter. Her fingers itched for a cigarette, but that was a no-no.

"What can I get for you, darlin'?"

She turned around to face the bartender, and her tongue tripped a little. He was tall, with wide shoulders and flashing blue eyes, wearing a pale-colored cowboy hat that screamed quality. A white dress shirt—Ike Behar if she had to guess—was tucked into dark slacks held onto a narrow waist with a nice belt. A large silver buckle with the initial "B" drew her gaze downward. When she glanced back to his face, his grin was wider. "I'm Boone. What's your name, pretty lady?"

"Carlotta," she said, giving herself a mental shake. Since when did she let a good looking buck tie her tongue? The guy couldn't be more than twenty-five.

"Nice to meet you, Carlotta. Is that an Atlanta accent I hear?"

She smiled. "You're good."

"That's what they tell me," he said with a wink. "Actually, my sister lives in Atlanta, so I've visited a time or two. What are you in the mood for tonight?" Then he ducked his chin. "To drink, I mean."

She laughed, warming up to his flirtation. It was a trick of his trade. "A glass of sauvignon blanc."

"House brand okay? It's pretty tasty."

"I'll take it... and a menu, please."

"Comin' right up."

He walked to the other end of the bar, then returned with a placemat and table setting which he arranged in front of her. From a refrigerator under the bar he removed a bottle of white wine and uncorked it expertly. Then he poured an inch into a glass and set it in front of her.

"See if you like it before you go all in."

She smirked at his innuendo, then swirled the clear liquid and lifted it to her mouth. The taste of grapefruit rolled over her tongue, and slid down her throat like a fresh shower. "Mm," she said, nodding. "It's very good."

"There's more where that came from," he said happily, then filled her glass and handed her a menu.

She scanned it, looking for something light. "Which of the small plates do you recommend?"

"The shrimp scampi is crazy good."

"I'll have that, please."

"Are you a guest of the hotel?"

She nodded and gave him her room number for the tab, then took a full sip of the wine. It was crazy good, too... or maybe she just needed the release... and a little fantasy to indulge in.

She watched the man move and gave in to a stir of appreciation. He was a stud, alright... and he knew it. Two scantily-clad women on the other end of the bar were drooling over him, and he was playing up to them. They were drinking martinis and rolling their tongues around the olive sticks. But Boone kept bouncing back to check on her, and she got the feeling he was sizing her up for a last-call tumble. And because the idea was shockingly appealing to her, Carlotta turned around on her stool to study the rest of the crowd. She intended to go to bed early—and alone.

It occurred to her that Patricia might have met her mystery man here for dinner, but she didn't see them in the crowd. Her phone vibrated from inside the purse on her lap. Carlotta removed it, hoping it wasn't more spammy dick pics. Instead it was a text from Patricia.

U were right about John. Happy?

Carlotta groaned. *What happened?*

I'll tell u tomorrow.

I'm at the restaurant bar if u want to come by. The bartender is cute.

No, thanks. Going to unpack.

I can come up if u want to talk.

But she didn't respond. Carlotta sighed.

"Not a happy message, I take it?" Boone asked.

She smiled, then shook her head. "No."

"Was it your boyfriend breaking up with you?"

Carlotta laughed. "No."

He leaned into the counter. "No, you don't have a boyfriend, or no, he didn't break up with you?"

She laughed. "Neither. It was my coworker. If my food will be a few minutes, I'd like to dash to take care of something. I won't be long."

"No problem. I'll save your seat."

Carlotta slid off the stool, then walked to the elevator and rode to the top floor. She would try to convince Patricia to come back to the bar with her. She owed her that much for their earlier disagreement—and for dissing her decision to meet the guy in the first place. Besides, she needed for her assistant to be in top form tomorrow, not moping over a catfish. She could at least be a shoulder for the woman to cry on and let her get it out of her system.

Walking to the end of the hallway where their rooms were located, Carlotta suddenly noticed how quiet it was. As she neared their doors, she could hear her own footsteps in the carpet. A shiver crawled up the back of her neck. She looked over her shoulder down the shadowy hall, but no one was following her... that she could see. She reached into her purse and frantically felt around for her phone, then yanked it out, her heart in her throat.

But she was alone.

Carlotta laughed at herself... when she was searching for her fugitive parents and moving bodies, she'd become accustomed to seeing a threat in every corner. She was past that now... her parents were home and she was an upwardly mobile career woman. There was no boogeyman here, only deadlines and expectations.

Stepping to Patricia's door, she knocked. "Patricia, it's me, Carlotta."

After a few seconds of silence passed, Carlotta knocked again. "Patricia? Why don't you come back to the bar with me and have a drink?"

When another few seconds passed, she sighed. "Okay, if you change your mind, you know where I am."

Carlotta backtracked to the bar, ridiculously pleased to see Boone had indeed saved her seat—with his cowboy hat. As she walked up, he was setting a plate of food on the placemat.

He grinned. "Perfect timing. Did you get whatever it was taken care of?"

"Yes," she said, then picked up his hat and handed it across the counter. "Thank you."

He took his hat, then frowned and wrapped his hand loosely around her wrist. "Hey, what happened?"

She glanced down to see a rivulet of blood dripping across the back of her hand and down her wrist. The business card holder—she must've scraped her hand against it when she rummaged for her phone. "Oh, it's just a scratch."

"That's a deep scratch," he said, then reached for a clean white towel and wrapped it around her hand.

She was mesmerized by his hands—the man was unbelievably sexy... and young... and sexy.

And young.

"There. At least it should stop the bleeding so you can eat." He winked. "But you can faint later and let me carry you back to your room."

All that muscle-bound youth in her bed... no strings. "I'm too old for you," she blurted.

He laughed. "How old do you think I am?"

"Twenty-five?"

"I'm thirty."

She studied his sexy smile. Was he lying?

Then he shrugged. "Just think about it, Carlotta, no pressure. Another glass of wine?"

"Uh-huh," she mumbled, as if she were in a trance.

He refilled her glass, then moved back down the bar to tend to the two tipsy girls, who shot daggers at Carlotta.

She took a drink of the wine, then dipped a fork into the shrimp scampi and savored one delicious bite before realizing a garlicky, greasy fish dish was probably not the best food to eat if she were going to have an illicit romp afterward. She set down her fork and took a drink of wine.

But she couldn't sleep with this guy.

She took another drink, then picked up her fork for another defiant bite of the scampi.

But he was scrumptious looking, to be sure.

She set down her fork and valiantly tried to remember if anything from the awful *Dating* magazine would help her in this situation. She swallowed another mouthful of wine, then pulled out her phone and texted Hannah.

U there?

Yeah, how's Dallas?

Hot, as in young cowboy bartender.

He wants to shake and stir u?

Yes.

And why are u texting me?

Should I?

Of fucking course!

I don't think I should.

Give me one reason and if u say Jack I'm going to have an aneurysm this second.

She pressed her lips together. *What if I said Coop?*

Shit. Then don't. He's worth it. But are u saying Coop?

I'm not saying.

U need counseling.

Carlotta frowned. *Bye.*

Fucking bye!

"How's your hand?" Boone asked.

She stowed her phone and held out her wrapped hand. "I think it stopped bleeding. Thank you."

"I have many talents," he said with a smile.

Carlotta sighed. "Unfortunately, I won't get to sample them."

He made a pouting face. "Darn. Can I ask how long you'll be in town?"

"A week."

He brightened. "So there's still a chance?"

She laughed, but shook her head no.

"Okay, my loss."

"Thanks for a fun evening," she said, then drank the last bit of wine. "And thanks for the towel."

Holding her wrapped hand, she turned and walked back to her room. She glanced at Patricia's door and nursed a pang of remorse for the woman who had a lot to offer, but who seemed unable to connect with people in a meaningful way.

Then with a start, she wondered if people thought the same about her.

She pulled up the app on her phone and punched in the code to open her door, relieved when it worked. When she entered the big, empty room, she walked to the picture window to look out over the twinkling lights of the skyline.

And just like that, she missed Atlanta... and the people there. One day in, and she was already homesick.

It was shaping up to be a long week.

Fatigue pulled at her. She went into the bathroom and took a quick shower to wash away the day, gingerly unwrapping the towel around her hand to rinse the angry scrape. She towel-dried her hair, donned a nightgown, and scheduled a wake-up call. Then she crawled into the luxurious covers and pulled them over her head.

To protect her from the boogeyman who was pursuing her down a long hallway. He was wearing a mask, and no matter how fast she ran, he was getting closer... and closer. When he grabbed her, she tore at the mask until it fell away... his face was black and white... the face in her locket... her real father—

A few minutes later a ringing noise woke her. Disoriented, she rolled over and felt on the nightstand for the phone receiver. Pain zinged through her hand. When she realized daylight streamed through the window and this was her wake up call, she groaned.

Hadn't she only just laid her head on the pillow?

She found the TV remote and turned on the news. Her hand throbbed from the scrape and her head throbbed from nicotine withdrawal. Surely it wouldn't hurt to lie there five... more... minutes...

The sound of a scream startled her awake. She sat straight up in bed, heart pounding, looking for the source, then realized it had come from the television. She exhaled, then her gaze landed on the clock and her pulse skyrocketed again. She'd overslept!

She levitated out of the bed and into the bathroom, in full-panic mode. The most important day of her career, and she was going to be late. She was supposed to meet Patricia twenty minutes ago... why hadn't she called?

Then Carlotta groaned. Because she'd probably overslept too! They were a pair.

She dialed Patricia's cell number while she brushed her teeth, but it rolled to voice mail.

Great.

"Patricia—" She spat in the sink. "It's Carlotta, are you up? I overslept. I'll meet you in the lobby as soon as I can. Text me if you get this."

She ended the call, then texted the manager of the Dallas salon. *A little unforeseen trouble this morning, running behind.*

Carlotta jumped under the shower for forty-five seconds. The scrape on her hand had crusted over, but she'd managed to break it open again. It hurt like hell, and looked worse. She hoped foundation would cover it.

Her head was pounding—she needed caffeine, but there was no time. Patricia hadn't yet texted her back, so she called again... and got her voicemail. She ended the call and texted *I'm running late... let me know when you get this.*

After slapping on minimal makeup, she jumped into a red Albert Nipon skirt suit she hadn't ironed, and yanked her dark hair back into a low ponytail. She felt nauseous as she gathered up her computer and the reports she'd studied and stuffed them into her bag. She was a scattered mess... she only hoped Patricia was faring better this morning.

She ran out the door still putting on her shoes. She hopped across the hall to Patricia's door, then knocked on it loudly. "Patricia? Patricia, are you awake?"

When there was no answer, Carlotta leaned in to put her ear against the door for signs of activity. When she heard none, she knocked again.

Carlotta backtracked into her room, then called the front desk and asked if a blond woman was waiting in the lobby.

"We don't see anyone, ma'am."

It suddenly occurred to her that Patricia might've gone to the meeting without her. As payback, to make her look bad?

She phoned the manager of the Dallas salon.

"Nedra English speaking."

"Nedra... this Carlotta Wren from the Atlanta store."

"Hello, Carlotta. I received your text that you're running behind."

"Yes, I apologize. I was wondering, has my assistant arrived yet?"

"Your assistant? No. But we're all here waiting. Lindy is on speaker phone."

"Hi, Carlotta," Lindy said. "Nedra tells me there's some trouble?"

Lindy sounded as if she weren't surprised. Carlotta closed her eyes. "I'll be there as soon as possible."

She ended the call, and went back to Patricia's door, not sure whether to be upset or concerned. Most likely, she'd taken another Xanax and was dead asleep. And while Carlotta was tempted to go to the meeting without her, she needed for her assistant to be there.

She pulled up the hotel app on her phone, then entered Patricia's room number, and squinted, trying to remember the code the woman had entered when showing Carlotta how to do it. 3-3-7-3? No... 3-3-7-6?

The green light flashed. Carlotta turned the handle and pushed open the door a few inches. "Patricia? Patricia, it's Carlotta. I'm sorry to barge in like this, but we're late for our meeting."

There was no sound, but remembering how the woman liked to wear earplugs, she walked in further. "Patricia?"

The door slammed closed behind her, jarring her nerves. She walked into the bedroom. The bed had been turned down, but not slept in. The sitting room was empty except for the remnants of a room service meal—for two.

She backtracked and walked to the bathroom door, which sat ajar. It was dark inside, but as soon as she pushed the door, the motion-sensing light came on, flooding the room.

Patricia lay sprawled on the floor wearing a Cat Lady nightshirt, face up with a pool of congealed blood around her blond head.

"Oh, no," Carlotta murmured, then rushed over and knelt down to see if she was still breathing.

She wasn't… and hadn't been for a while.

Carlotta pulled out her phone with a shaking hand and tapped 9-1-1.

"9-1-1, what's the address of your emergency?"

Carlotta gave the address, trying to stay calm despite her pounding pulse.

"And what's your emergency?"

"A guest of the Saxler House hotel has died. Please send the coroner."

"Right away. And the police will be summoned, too. What is your name, ma'am?"

"Carlotta Wren." She spelled her last name. "I found the body."

"Are you in danger, ma'am?"

"No."

"I'll need for you to stay with the victim and on the line with me until the police get there."

"Okay, but I'm going to put you on hold. I have another call to make."

"But—"

Carlotta tapped the hold button, then pushed to her feet and tapped in a phone number by heart.

Jack Terry answered on the second ring. "Hi, Carlotta. So you are still alive. What's up?"

Her heart gave a little squeeze at the comforting sound of his voice. "Hi, Jack. I'm in Dallas on a business trip."

"Oh, nice. I was afraid you were calling about a body."

"Um… as a matter of fact…"

His groan sounded over the phone. "I was joking. Are you alright?"

"A little shaken up," she admitted. "It's my coworker Patricia Alexander. I just found her dead in her hotel room."

"What happened?"

"Hard to say, a head wound, I think. She's on the bathroom floor. I already called 9-1-1, so the police are on the way. Will the APD get involved?"

"No, probably not."

Her spirits sagged a little. "Okay."

"But yours truly will be there as soon as I can arrange a flight. Sit tight."

Carlotta smiled into the phone. "Bye, Jack."

CHAPTER 6

WES'S FOREHEAD hit the counter with a *blam*! He jerked back, over-compensated, and threw himself off the stool he was sitting on, cracking his head against the tile. He lay on the floor of the Lindbergh Family Driving Range—Where winners are made!— seeing stars.

"Fuck!"

"You okay, son?"

He winced and opened his eyes to see his father standing over him. Nodding against the pain he reached up to palpate a goose egg on the back of his noggin. "I think so."

"What happened?"

"I guess I fell asleep."

Randolph frowned. "You need to be more disciplined about your schedule."

Wes gingerly pushed to his feet. "I was up late playing video poker."

"It's good that you're practicing, but I'm counting on you to open the shop most mornings, at least until we find someone to help out." He gestured to the Help Wanted flyer posted on the window. "Don't you know some kids your age at that city job who are looking to move up in the world?"

"The kids I work with are super smart—they all attend Georgia Tech."

Randolph gave a sharp laugh. "How smart could they be if they're working for the city?" He gestured vaguely to the unkempt twenty acres or so extending from the tees. "I know this doesn't look like much yet, but I have big plans for this place, and it'll be yours someday."

Wes conjured up a flat smile. "Great."

"Try to stay awake, okay?"

Wes nodded. "I'll do better."

"And watch your language," his dad added. "We want to attract a high class customer here."

Meaning, of course, he was low-class. Wes watched his dad walk from the lobby out onto the range tee carrying two little buckets of balls. Randolph extended a smile to the two men standing there, decked out head to toe in the sissiest golf clothes imaginable, but oozing money. His dad engaged them in conversation, eliciting a few laughs, then offered them the extra balls. The complimentary golf balls amounted to pennies, but his dad knew it would make the geezers feel special, and they'd be back soon to spend more money.

Wes glanced at the clock and groaned. Forty minutes into his new job and he already hated it—hated golf lingo, hated the people who played golf, hated the people who made effing golf balls.

With Meg off galivanting her way across Europe, this was shaping up to be the most miserable summer of his life.

The urge to take a hit of Oxy rose up in his chest like a tide... he could picture the little white pills suspended in ice in his freezer at home, just waiting to be liberated so they could make him feel amazing. He'd stared at them this morning for an entire two minutes before closing the freezer door.

He shuffled over to the coffee station, poured himself a cup, and added a shitload of sugar. The ten hours left on his shift stretched out like an eternity.

And tomorrow he got to get up at the buttcrack of dawn and do it all over again.

He took a drink of the coffee and burned his tongue. "Fuuuuuuck!" He lifted his arm to smash the cup and its contents against the freshly painted wall.

"Hey, Little Man, what's up?"

Stopping mid-motion, he turned his head to see Mouse standing in the doorway dressed in a bad blue suit, holding a familiar golf club, fondly referred to as The Collector. Wes grinned. "Mouse!"

He almost hugged the big man, but at the last minute caught himself and extended his fist for a bump. Mouse laughed and obliged. "I thought I'd come and check out your new digs."

The man glanced around the long, narrow room that resembled a bar, except behind the counter were bins holding buckets of golf balls and little net bags of tees. A small merchandising area offered balls, tees, gloves, towels, and bottled water for sale. And a coffee station, which his dad kept stocked with the blackest, most bitter coffee ever.

"It's pretty bleak," Wes offered.

"Nah... it's old school," Mouse said, trying to put a good spin on it.

"Dad wants to update everything, but I'm not sure he knows what to do first."

"Looks like he got the uniform right."

Wes frowned down at his bright green golf shirt and pleated khaki pants. "I look like a wuss."

Mouse laughed, then nodded toward the window looking onto the range tee where Randolph was still passing out free balls. "Is that your dad?"

"Yeah."

"You look like him... and not just because you're both wearing the same wussy outfit."

Wes laughed. "That's what everyone says, but I don't see it." Then he gestured to the club Mouse was holding. "You out collecting today?"

"Naw... I'm not doing so much for The Carver these days."

"What are you doing?"

Mouse shrugged. "This and that."

Wes took the cue not to ask for details.

"Hey, how's that little girlfriend of yours?"

Wes frowned. "Meg's in Germany for the summer."

"But you still talk and stuff?"

"Yeah, we Skype and text, but the time difference is a pain."

"Ah. Well, you know what they say—absence makes the heart grow fonder."

"Yeah, but it's murder on the balls."

Mouse laughed heartily and Wes joined in.

"Wesley?"

He looked up to see Randolph had returned.

"Who's your friend?"

Wes straightened. "Dad, this is Mouse. We used to... work together."

"Nice to meet you, Mr. Wren," Mouse said, extending a big beefy paw.

Randolph shook his hand warily. "I didn't catch your last name, Mouse."

The big man shrugged good-naturedly. "Mouse is enough."

His dad's jaw tightened. "Are you one of Hollis Carver's guys?"

"Used to be."

"What do you do now?"

"I guess you could say I'm an independent contractor."

Randolph gave a curt nod. "Are you a golfer, Mouse?"

"Some. Wes and I had fun playing a time or two."

His father's surprised gaze bounced to him. "Really?"

"Mouse bought me the driver you admired," Wes offered.

"That was nice of you," Randolph said to Mouse.

"Wes is easy to be nice to. He's a good man."

"Thank you," Randolph said, then smiled.

"That's a compliment for Wes," Mouse said mildly.

Wes watched his father's face darken, then Mouse turned to him.

"So, Wes, are you going to sell me a bucket of balls or not?"

Wes walked back to the counter. "Sure, Mouse."

"Here's a bucket on the house," Randolph said, extending the much smaller container. "You look as though you're taking a break from your job and will want to get back right away."

Tension crackled between the two men, locked in a stare-down. Wes swallowed hard.

Mouse held up his hand and smiled. "Thanks, but no thanks. I pay my way." He walked to the counter and laid down a fifty dollar bill. "Will that buy a couple of buckets?"

"Sure," Wes said. "And change."

"Great. And maybe your dad will spot you long enough to come out and hit a couple of balls with me?"

Wes looked to his dad, who nodded, but did not look happy.

Wes handed a bucket over the counter to Mouse, who moved toward the door exiting to the tee. Wes picked up the other bucket and started to follow. But when the door closed behind Mouse, his dad spoke.

"*Wesley.*"

Wes swallowed and turned back.

"I don't want that man coming around here again."

Wes frowned. "But he's my friend."

"He's a thug. Look at him, he's ridiculous."

Anger spiked in Wes's chest, making him more brave than smart. "Mouse looked out for me. He saved my ass more than once… when *you* weren't around."

Randolph's jaw hardened, but he didn't respond.

Wes turned toward the door and walked out, his feet lighter than they'd felt all morning.

CHAPTER 7

CARLOTTA PACED a waiting room in the Dallas Police Department, nursing a cup of lukewarm coffee. Her hand shook. She was deep in the throes of nicotine withdrawal—she'd been in too big of a rush to put on a fresh transdermal patch this morning, and then all hell had broken loose. She walked up to a window and waved to capture the attention of the uniformed officer standing nearby.

"Excuse me, is there a cigarette machine in the building?"

"Nope." He barely looked at her as he recited in monotone, "No smoking on the premises, ma'am."

She frowned. "That seems like a poorly thought-out rule for a place of high stress."

"It's not a rule, ma'am, it's a law."

She smothered a groan. "Could you please remind someone I'm waiting?"

"Sure. And who are you?"

Tamping down her frustration, she said, "My name is Carlotta Wren. I'm waiting to give a statement about the guest who died at the Saxler House hotel. The detective at the scene was Nadine Lawson. She asked me to come, and I've been here for almost three hours."

"Okie, doke, have a seat."

She expelled a sigh and continued to pace, too wired to sit. Her phone buzzed with a text from Hannah.

How are u holding up?

I could use a smoke. No developments.

Shit. I wasn't crazy about Patricia, but shit.

I know. Hey, thanks for getting Jack a room on such short notice.

Anything to keep him out of your room.

Carlotta smirked. *Later.*

Hang in there.

Carlotta paced to the far end of the room, then back, in an attempt to walk off her nervous energy. She couldn't believe Patricia was dead... had probably lain on the bathroom floor all night while other guests—including her—strolled by her room. She stopped and put a hand to her aching temple. She couldn't think straight... she needed... she needed...

Her phone rang and she was relieved to see Jack's name on the screen. Apparently that was what she needed.

"Jack? Where are you?"

"Taxi just dropped me at the main DPD station. I'm in the lobby. Where are you?"

"Still waiting to give a statement. Second floor."

"I see the stairs."

She squinted, trying to remember the layout. "At the top, there's an American flag display in the hallway, then turn right."

"Nice suit. You always look good in red."

She turned around and saw him in the doorway, his shoulders spanning the frame. He wore jeans, a tucked-in shirt, and a sport coat, and his trademark black boots were in step with the local fashion. In one hand he held a leather duffle bag, in the other he held his phone to his ear. Her traitorous heart did a handstand. She smiled and lowered her phone.

He smiled and lowered his phone.

She didn't care what it looked like or how he interpreted it, she walked into his arms and pressed her face against his chest. She clung to him and relived all the emotions he'd made her feel since she'd last lain in his arms—heartache over his betrayal with Liz, gratitude for keeping her mother's location in Vegas a secret, sorrow that he had to arrest Liz himself for her evil deeds, relief that a child wouldn't be born into a terrible situation, and bewilderment that he wouldn't tell her himself that he was free.

He didn't say anything, just tucked her head under his chin and held her close.

When she realized they were garnering attention, she pulled back and untangled herself from his big body. "Thank you for coming."

"I had a couple of personal days, and it seemed like a good time to get away."

She nodded. He probably felt as if he'd walked through a fire and lived to tell about it.

"I brought you something," he said.

"What?"

He held his finger to his lips, then reached into his inside coat pocket and removed a pack of cigarettes—menthols.

She gasped in delight. "Oh, Jack, I love you!"

They both froze, and she realized with horror what she'd said.

"For... remembering my favorite brand," she continued brightly.

His lips parted and she could tell his mind was racing for a response.

"Carlotta Wren?" drawled a female voice.

She turned to see the dark-haired female detective who'd been on the scene at the hotel holding a file folder. "I'm here."

The woman looked over and smiled. "Yes, we met briefly this morning. I'm Detective Lawson." Her gaze flitted to Jack—the entire length of him.

Jack extended his hand. "Detective Jack Terry, Atlanta PD."

She shook his hand. "APD is involved?"

"No. This is... personal interest," he said.

Her gaze bounced back and forth between them.

"We're not together," they said in unison, then looked at each other.

"We're just friends," Carlotta offered quickly.

The detective squinted. "Okay. Ms. Wren, if you'll follow me, I have some questions to ask you about the deceased."

"Can Jack accompany me?"

"Of course," the woman said with a little smile. "Professional courtesy and all that."

"I presented my weapon at the front desk," Jack offered. "It's in my duffel, unloaded."

"Thanks for the heads up, Detective. This way."

They followed her down a long hallway to a secure door she badged through, then past a bull-pen of desks and cubicles into a small private room with a table and four chairs. Carlotta sat on one side of the table and the female detective sat opposite her. Jack sat at the end, perhaps to indicate he was a neutral observer.

"Sorry for the wait," she said to Carlotta. "It always takes longer to process a scene in a public place. Hopefully we can get through this part quickly."

Carlotta nodded. "I'll tell you what I can."

"First, I'm very sorry for your loss. How did you know Patricia Alexander?"

"We're coworkers at Neiman Marcus in Atlanta. We were in Dallas on business, to work with the downtown location."

From the file, she picked up a business card. "It says you are the Director of the Atlanta Bridal Salon?"

"Yes."

"Hm. I thought the salon here in Dallas was the only one."

"The Atlanta salon won't open until this fall. Patricia and I were here to learn from our counterparts."

"And Ms. Alexander was your assistant?"

Was. "That's right."

"And when did you arrive?"

"Yesterday, late afternoon."

The detective took down the airline information.

"And what led you to find Ms. Alexander's body this morning?"

"We had a meeting, and she didn't show at the arranged time. When she didn't respond to my texts or my calls, I began to worry."

"And how did you access her room?"

"With the hotel app on my phone. Patricia helped me to set it up, so I knew her access code."

"And you found the body lying face-up in the bathroom?"

"Yes."

"Did you touch anything?"

Jack coughed—as a warning?

"I checked to see if she was breathing, but I could tell she'd been deceased for a while."

"Oh? And how could you tell?"

"The blood around her head was congealed. Also, rigor mortis had set in, and liver mortis was noticeable on her arms, legs, and the right side of her face that was turned toward the floor."

Detective Lawson's eyebrows climbed and she shot a look at Jack.

"Carlotta's not your average shop girl," he offered.

"I sometimes work for the morgue," Carlotta added. "Moving bodies."

The woman pursed her mouth. "I see. Okay, well, thank you for the detail. From the scene, it looks as if Ms. Alexander fell and hit her head on the floor with enough force to fracture the skull."

"That's unusual, isn't it?" Carlotta asked.

"Yes, but it happens. Especially if the victim passed out and fell hard. Do you know if Ms. Alexander was taking any medication?"

"She took Xanax before she got on the plane."

"Yes, we found that prescription bottle. So Ms. Alexander was probably under the influence of the tranquilizer and simply passed out. The toxicology report will help us to confirm the cause of death." She closed the file. "Thank you for coming in." The woman started to stand.

"Wait a minute," Carlotta said, lifting her hand. "Before you classify the death as an accident, you should know Patricia was supposed to have dinner last night with a man she met online, and I noticed there were two room service meals on her table."

Detective Lawson seemed unfazed. "You think this man might've had something to do with her death?"

Carlotta wet her lips. "I also noticed marks on her throat. They were very faint, but they could've been from fingers."

The woman's eyebrows climbed. "You think she was strangled by this man she met online?"

"I simply think you should be open to all possibilities."

The detective shifted in her chair, not happy to be upbraided. "Do you know this man's name?"

"Patricia said it was John Smythe."

Detective Lawson pursed her mouth. "Really?"

"I had the same reaction when she told me, but she said his last name was spelled with a 'y' and an 'e' on the end... to her that seemed legitimate."

Detective Lawson's mouth went flat. "Did you hear from her after the dinner date?"

"She sent me a text that I was right about him, and that she'd tell me about it today."

The woman smirked. "So she obviously survived the date."

"But what if he came back to her room?"

She looked dubious. "I'll make a note of it."

But Carlotta noticed she didn't. "Did you find Patricia's cell phone?" she pressed.

"We weren't looking for it."

Carlotta bit her tongue. *She* had looked for it before the police arrived, and couldn't locate it—not in the bathroom, not in Patricia's purse or her luggage. But then, Patricia herself admitted she misplaced her phone often. She could've carried it to the ice machine room and left it, or run an errand and lost it in the process.

"Was there something else you wanted to add?" the detective said, obviously humoring her.

"There was a man at the taxi kiosk at the airport who flirted with Patricia. She gave him her business card."

"And your theory there?"

"She might've called him after the date with John Smythe went south."

"Okay," the detective said. "I'll make a note of it."

Yet she didn't. "The guy at the airport was about six-one, one hundred eighty pounds, brown hair, green eyes, and he had a smashed thumbnail."

Detective Lawson bounced her gaze to Jack, who simply lifted his hands in a "welcome to my world" gesture.

Carlotta shot him a frown, then looked back to the Dallas detective. "What will happen to her personal property?"

"When the police release the room back to the hotel, her things will be boxed up and shipped to her next of kin." The Detective's Apple watch buzzed. She glanced at it, then gave them an apologetic smile. "I need to be somewhere, but I think we're finished here. When will you be returning to Atlanta, Ms. Wren?"

"Tomorrow." Out of respect, Lindy had postponed the meetings, which made sense logistically, too, since Carlotta would need a new assistant to sit in on the meetings with her.

"Safe travels back, and again, I'm sorry about your friend."

Carlotta recalled Patricia's words on the plane.

We're not friends.

"Thank you," Carlotta murmured.

"My apologies, but can you find your way out?"

Jack nodded, then stood.

"Detective," she said with a dip of her chin, then left the room.

Carlotta frowned at Jack. "You were a lot of help."

"Hey, I brought you cigarettes. Let's let you go smoke one so you can get in a better mood."

"I've already been warned about smoking on the premises."

"And that stopped you?"

"Not having a cigarette stopped me."

"I saw a park a couple of blocks away. Let's stretch our legs."

He picked up his duffle bag, then waited for her to precede him through the door. Jack was always gentlemanly... if you didn't count the sleeping with other women thing.

Although, if pressed, he would probably point out it was more gentlemanly not to talk about his extracurricular activities.

The man was a conundrum.

She walked out with him, and they were immediately blasted by the intense heat of the sun.

"God, it's hot here," he said, shrugging out of his jacket.

"Homesick already?" she teased.

"No, it's good to get away, actually." Then he made a thoughtful noise. "I'm really sorry about your coworker, though."

She nodded. "I can't believe just yesterday Patricia was alive and walking around and planning to live a long life. I guess you just never know when your time is up."

"So true," he agreed. "A job like mine makes a person immune to the impact of crime, until it happens to someone I'm close to."

"Like Maria?"

He nodded. Maria Marquez had been Jack's partner at one point, and had been murdered by the ex-husband she'd moved to Atlanta to avoid. Carlotta had been jealous of her exotic beauty and proximity to Jack, which seemed so petty now. She knew the woman's death still weighed on Jack's mind.

They walked in companionable silence to the entrance of a small park that had been ensconced in the center of a city block. It was a popular place and all the benches were taken up by readers or people eating a bag lunch.

Jack gestured to a shady spot in the grass under a large live oak. "You can sit on my jacket if you don't mind being on the ground."

"Sounds good."

They waded through ankle-high grass, then he spread his jacket over a level spot. She kicked off her pumps and situated herself, heaving a long sigh. "That feels good."

He lowered himself in the grass next to her and nodded. "And we're far enough away from everyone else that you can enjoy a cigarette."

She grinned and pulled out the pack to tear open the cellophane. Even this part of the ritual was soothing.

"Hey, what happened to your hand?"

She glanced down at the line of raw red skin still visible under the foundation she'd applied to conceal it. "It's nothing. Do you have a lighter?"

"Nope. I thought you would."

Her shoulders fell. "I've been trying to quit these things. Do you have matches?"

"Sorry."

She made a frustrated noise that even to her own ears sounded like Priscilla when she didn't get her way.

"Give me your phone," he said.

"Are you going to have Amazon fly by and drop a lighter with a drone?"

He laughed. "No. Put the cigarette in your mouth and lean out into the sun."

Dubious, she followed his instructions, squinting into the blinding heat. Then he held her dark phone screen in front of the cigarette, and adjusted the angle.

"Draw on it," he said.

She did and was rewarded with a curl of smoke at the end. She gasped. "How did you know how to do that?"

He handed back her phone. "I was a Boy Scout."

"I believe that," she said with a laugh, drawing deeply on the cigarette. "Oh, God, this tastes so good." She exhaled, then looked over at him. "You're not going to lecture me about smoking?"

"No. You know it's bad for you."

"Old habits die hard, and all that jazz."

"Yep."

She knew he was thinking about their habit of falling together, then rebounding off each other and coming back for more.

"I guess you heard Liz isn't going to have a baby," he said quietly.

She drew on the cigarette, then exhaled slowly. "I did. But it would've been nice to hear it from you."

He looked over. "I didn't think you'd care. And frankly, I was ashamed of how relieved I was."

"There's no shame in not wanting a child to be born into such a troubled situation. How is Liz?"

"Not well," he said gravely. "Maybe not even well enough to stand trial."

"She's in a psychiatric facility?"

"Right. And unless something changes, she might be there the rest of her life."

"I'm sorry she wasn't the woman you thought she was."

Jack made a somber noise. "Liz and I were far from the ideal couple, but I thought we'd be able to co-parent. After I wrapped my head around being a father, I was sort of looking forward to it. Now... I don't know what my role is supposed to be. I don't want to just abandon her."

"I know. I feel the same way about Peter."

"What's going on with his case?"

"Stalled. His attorney keeps hoping to get him out on bail, but Walt Tully's attempt to flee has labeled all of them a flight risk."

"Too bad," Jack said. "No offense, but Peter doesn't seem like the type who will flourish in captivity."

"Can't disagree with you there. Peter's upbringing didn't prepare him for adversity."

He grunted. "Speaking of, how are things with your family? Is your mother improving?"

She nodded, but took another drag to postpone her response. "Things are fine. My mother is much improved and they're moving to a new house soon."

"That's probably good."

"Yes... that house holds too many memories."

"Are you moving with them?"

"No. I moved back to the townhouse with Wes. He and Randolph have been fixing it up. And Randolph bought a driving range in Lindbergh. Wesley is working with him."

"That's nice. Wes is staying out of trouble?"

She held up crossed fingers. "And we're still waiting to hear about the charges he racked up in Vegas. Kelvin Lucas is supposed to be going to bat for Wes, but with Liz out of the picture, he has to retain a new attorney."

"It'll all work out," he said in a voice that made her believe it. "And how's Prissy?"

Carlotta scoffed. "Living up to her name. She adores the puppy you gave her. But wow, that girl is a handful."

He belly-laughed. "If that's not the pot calling the kettle black, I don't know what is. It's obvious the two of you are sisters, looks and otherwise."

Half-sisters, as it turns out.

"How are things between you and your dad?" he asked.

She averted her gaze. "Fine." Then she took a final draw on the cigarette, pulling it down to the filter.

"Only fine?"

She shrugged and stubbed out the cigarette butt. "We don't see each other much now that I'm not living there. And he seems to have charmed his way back into Buckhead society."

Carlotta felt Jack's inquisitive golden eyes boring into her, watching her. She flirted with the idea of telling him Randolph wasn't her father, but she'd promised her parents not to tell anyone outside the family. And Jack had a history of coming and going from her life. He was sitting with her now... but how soon before he went off on his own again? She couldn't risk sharing a secret of that magnitude with someone who wasn't invested in her happiness.

She busied herself looking for a mint, then popped it into her mouth. "Come on... let's get you checked into the hotel and have some dinner. I'm starving."

"I'll call an Uber." But he didn't move, seemed to be focused on her lips.

She licked them. "Why, Jack, I do believe you're embracing modern technology. The next thing I know, you'll be Instagramming me."

He leaned into her, his mouth mere inches from hers. "Is that something dirty?"

She swallowed the mint. "Jack..."

He searched her eyes and she could see the war raging in his. He wanted her... but he didn't want to want her. Everything he'd ever shared with her—including his body—had been done reluctantly. And she didn't want to be an impulse he was constantly fighting.

She pulled back and pushed to her feet. "I'll get Prissy to teach you about social media sometime. She's a whiz. And since she's announced she's going to marry you, you'll need to get up to speed."

He laughed and slowly got to his feet, then pulled out his phone and summoned a car. Her light-hearted subject change had put them back on friendly territory as they strolled to the sidewalk to wait for their ride.

"So you're a director now, huh?" he asked.

She smiled. "Yes. The general manager put me in charge of the new salon, and it came with a title."

"And an assistant, very nice."

"Not so nice for Patricia, as it turned out."

"Hey... none of this is your fault. And I know how you like to turn every death into a movie of the week," he said dryly, "but chances are, it happened the way Detective Lawson said it did. Patricia was probably upset over the failed dinner date, took something to feel better, then passed out and hit the floor too hard. It's tragic, but it happens—and it happens more often than people are murdered." He gave her a pointed look. "Let it go."

She knew Jack was right... and she wanted to believe it was an accident. But she'd never forgive herself if she didn't follow up on every detail of Patricia's death—she owed the woman that much.

When the car arrived, they slid into the backseat and Jack casually draped his arm around her shoulder. They chatted about the passing scenery and current events, and she realized this was the most relaxed she'd ever seen the man. She wished they could stay in this protective cocoon longer—she might actually learn something about him.

And it made her apprehensive to think about where he would wind up sleeping tonight. She had schooled herself to resist Alpha Jack with the big ego and the swagger. But Beta Jack... that was a whole new temptation.

"Wow," he said when they pulled up to the hotel. "Hannah's family owns this place?"

"And many more."

"So which is the real Hannah—the tatted Goth-chick, or the Heiress to an Empire?"

"She prefers the tatted version, but she plays the role of social climber to appease her father. And honestly, she can pull off both."

He seemed doubly impressed when they walked inside the building. Carlotta stood nearby as he checked in.

"I'm sorry we don't have a room closer to Ms. Wren's," the clerk said. "The only room available is on the second floor." She winced apologetically. "In fact, it's about as far away as possible."

Carlotta smothered a smile. *Loud and clear, Hannah.*

"That's fine," Jack assured the woman.

"Ms. Wren, our deepest condolences on the passing of your friend."

"Thank you," Carlotta murmured.

"If we find her cell phone, what should we do with it?"

Carlotta squinted. "Excuse me?"

"Ms. Alexander called the desk last night to say she'd misplaced her phone, and wanted us to be on the lookout for it."

She felt Jack's I-told-you-so gaze on her as she fished a business card out of her purse. "If it turns up, call me."

She led Jack to the elevator.

"If her phone is found," he said, "don't you think it should be handed over to Detective Lawson?"

"Why? Patricia died accidentally, remember?"

"Her family, then."

"I'll make sure they get it—after I check it and remove any business data."

"Yeah, there's so much bridal shop espionage going on, you can't be too careful."

She frowned at him, then pushed the button for her floor. He pushed the button for his floor. They were *sooooo* far apart.

"What time would you like to have dinner?" he asked.

"After the world's longest shower," she said. "And maybe a nap."

The door opened onto his floor. "Ping me when you're ready."

She nodded, then rode to the top floor. When she alighted, she had the same eerie feeling as the night before. The silence was oppressive. She walked quickly to her door, sending a brief look toward Patricia's room. A Closed for Housekeeping sign had been posted. Otherwise, there was no indication someone had died there. She fumbled to open the door to her room, and once inside, heaved a sigh of relief.

She kicked off her shoes, and opted for the nap before the shower. Thankfully she was too exhausted for the troubling dreams of the night before. When her phone alarm went off, she felt much refreshed, and a long cool shower revived her. She picked up her phone and pinged Jack.

Meet u in the lobby in 30 min?

Sounds good.

She smiled at the friendly exchange, thinking maybe they could dine and later say goodnight without the of haze of sexual awareness hanging over them.

That said, she acknowledged a tickle of anticipation to be spending the evening with Jack, just the two of them, like a normal, ordinary, regular couple.

Who were friends.

Carlotta surveyed her limited wardrobe choices, settling on a loose black Eileen Fisher dress with the lavender scarf for a pop of color, and silver-colored sandals. She skipped foundation and focused on making up her brown eyes. Cherry red lipstick highlighted the gap between her front teeth, but she liked the effect.

And the way Jack's eyes lit up when he saw her, she assumed he liked the effect, too.

"You look good," he said.

"So do you." He wore an ivory-colored dress shirt tucked into dress jeans, and a black jacket. The man was tall and wide and devastatingly male. All the women—and half of the men—working the front desk followed him with their eyes.

77

"Did you get your nap?"

"I did. What did you do?"

"I went for a run, then hit the pool for some laps."

"Is that where you get your year-round tan—by a pool?" She knew so little about Jack's life.

"Hardly," he said. "Do you have a place in mind for dinner?"

She noticed his subtle deflection. "Not really."

"The concierge suggested a steak and seafood place within walking distance. Are you game?"

"Sure."

The temperature had cooled a few degrees, making the walk pleasant. Jack told her a story about Brooklyn, the female dispatcher at the precinct Carlotta knew. She laughed and glanced up at him while he talked, reveling in the luxury of having him to herself for the evening. He seemed to be in a good mood, and she surmised that having the weight of an impending child—with an unstable mother—off his mind had much to do with it. Maybe the near-brush with a life he didn't want had made him reevaluate and consider the life he did want.

But if so, how would it fit with the life she wanted?

They were able to maintain their playful banter over dinner and even touched on more serious topics. Politics seemed uppermost on everyone's mind these days, and Jack had concerns about how different candidates framed their views on crime. After years in law enforcement, he wanted to see more resources devoted to soft prevention methods, like improved neighborhood lighting, and intervention for minor violations to prevent young offenders from sliding into a career of crime.

Carlotta drank from her wine glass and observed him, open and animated, like she'd never seen him before. She liked this side of him—dangerously so. Desire curled low in her stomach, driven by the fact that she knew *that* side of him very well. She and Jack had always been in synch between the sheets.

Walking back to the hotel, she could feel their attraction reverberating back and forth and building with every step, every brush of their hands, every sigh.

"I'll walk you to your room," he said casually.

"Okay," she agreed, just as casually. But her heart was thumping like a drum during the elevator ride. They were both quiet, looking up at the ceiling, or down at the floor. When the bell dinged and the doors opened, they stepped out and she gestured toward her room. "At the end of the hall."

"Nice," he said, glancing around. "I assume Hannah set you up with a penthouse suite?"

"She did."

Her breath quickened as they walked up to her door. She used the electronic key to open the lock, then turned back. "Thanks for dinner, Jack."

"It was nice," he agreed.

She raised up on her toes and kissed him on the mouth, a quick peck. But before she could pull back, he had captured her mouth in a proper open-mouth, tongue-on-tongue kiss. Her body leapt in remembrance, urging her on. She looped her arms around his neck, and he ran his hands down her back, pulling her soft hollows to his hardened hills. Alarms sounded in her head.

Warning! Warning! Man on the rebound! No commitment ahead!

She pulled back and looked into his hooded eyes. "Jack…"

"Uh-hm?"

"Where do you live?"

He blinked. "Hm?"

"Your address. Where do you live? And is it an apartment or a house?"

"Uh…" He straightened. "Is that important right now?"

She crossed her arms. "And one day when you came to the Buckhead house, you told me there were things you didn't tell me when you should have. What did you mean?"

"Uh… hm, I'm not sure." He pulled his big hand down his face. "Did I say that?"

Carlotta's heart shivered. "Yes, you did." Here she'd been spinning fantasies that he'd been trying to say he'd loved her all along, and he couldn't even remember saying it.

He squinted. "Are you sure?"

Tears pressed on the back of her eyes. Before she made a complete fool of herself, she said, "Goodnight, Jack." She wasn't angry, she wasn't hurt… just resigned.

And *done.*

He pressed his lips together. "I did something wrong, didn't I?"

She managed a little smile. "No. It's fine... we're fine. Breakfast in the hotel restaurant tomorrow?"

"Uh... sure."

"Around ten? Then we can leave for the airport and get back to reality."

He seemed a little dazed, but nodded. "Okay... goodnight, Carlotta."

"Goodnight, Jack."

She pushed open the door to her room, slipped inside, then closed it with a solid *click*. She leaned against the door, willing him to knock and apologize and share even a few details about his life.

Instead she heard him step away from the door and the sound of his footsteps recede. She turned to look out the peephole and sure enough, the fisheye lens showed him walking away. The distant sound of the elevator bell reached her, the doors opening... closing.

Carlotta sighed. But this was better than spending a night in his arms, then going back to Atlanta and resuming their gray relationship category of "it's complicated."

She pushed away from the door, knowing she'd made the right decision. She'd been guilty in the past of not expecting more from Jack, and look where it had gotten her—confused and unable to open her heart to anyone else.

Ack, relationships were so hard... no wonder so many women took their chances with strangers they met online.

And the more she thought about the interview with Detective Lawson, the more sour she became. The woman seemed determined to stamp Patricia's death an accident, when there were other possibilities. Carlotta bit into her lip. Once she returned to Atlanta, she could talk to Coop about performing an autopsy.

But once she left the potential crime scene, she'd be limited to her memory.

A situation she might be able to remedy now.

Carlotta looked through the peephole to make sure the hallway was empty, then opened the door and walked across the hall to

Patricia's room. She held up her phone. Had the police and hotel staff been careless enough to leave the access code the same?

A green light flashed on the lock—they had.

With her pulse clicking double-time, she pushed open the door and stepped inside. Moonlight shone through the glass wall, illuminating her way until her movements triggered the overhead lights to turn on. The room remained much the state she'd seen it this morning—the bed turned down but unslept in, and Patricia's belongings throughout the bedroom and the bathroom. This time she took pictures of everything, panoramic-style. The woman's suitcases were open on valet stands, both of them half-empty. She remembered Patricia's text that she was going to unpack—it was sad to think she'd been doing something so mundane when she'd died.

Carlotta moved to the bathroom, wincing at the bloodstain on the floor, and the outline inside it showing where she'd lain. On the vanity sat Patricia's large black makeup case, and around it an array of beauty products, many of them brands she didn't recognize. Some of them were toppled, indicating Patricia might have scattered them when she fell.

Using the end of her scarf, Carlotta carefully unzipped the luxurious makeup case, admired its beautifully arranged products, all top brands sold at Neiman's, then rezipped it. Again, she took a panoramic picture, splicing together shots as she moved the phone lens, just the way Prissy had taught her. When she turned to leave the bathroom, she noticed a small trash can under the vanity and nudged it out with her foot to see if anything was inside. It was empty... but the movement dislodged a plastic baggie that had been wedged between the trash can and the wall.

She snapped a picture of the baggie, then picked it up the by the corner, expecting to find pills or maybe the remnants of a toiletry inside. Instead, it was a condom.

Ew. Carlotta winced, but resisted the impulse to drop the baggie and its contents. If one of the two men Patricia had been in contact with had been involved in her death, this might be the evidence needed to prove they were here. She took a picture of the baggie, noting it was sealed.

She pondered calling the police station and leaving a message for Detective Lawson... and telling her what? That she'd decided to go back to the scene and dig around a little more? The woman was already convinced she was a troublemaker.

She considered calling Jack, but that was worse—he was on Lawson's side, and would accuse her of trying to prove a crime that hadn't been committed.

And chances were, Lawson and Jack were right. Who knew how long the condom had been there? There was no sign of activity on the bed to indicate Patricia had had sex, so it followed the condom probably didn't belong to either of her two men.

Carlotta held it over the trash can to dispose of it, then at the last second, she decided to wrap it in a tissue and put it in her purse.

Once Lawson told her the case was closed, she'd dispose of it.

She pushed to her feet, suddenly eager to get away from the place where Patricia had taken her last breath. She moved to the door and looked out the peephole to make sure the hallway was clear.

And saw Jack walking toward her door.

She inhaled sharply, and her heartrate spiked. What was this about?

From her viewpoint, she could see him clearly. His back was to her as he stood in front of the room she was staying in. Then he turned around and she could see his face. He looked worried... torn... uncertain. Then he turned back to her door, lifted his hand, and knocked.

She grimaced. When she didn't answer, he'd think she was blowing him off. If she came out of Patricia's room, the jig was up and he'd be so angry, he'd probably leave anyway. And report her to Lawson.

"Carlotta," he called. "Are you there? I just want to... talk."

While her heart did gymnastics, he seemed to change his mind and started to leave, then he came back. Then he pulled his hand over his mouth, turned, and strode away.

The distant sound of the elevator ding reached her. The doors opening... then closing. Her shoulders fell.

Carlotta waited a few seconds, then quietly opened the door, slipped out, and closed the door behind her. Then she race-walked across the hall to her own room and got inside as quickly as she could. She slid down the door and sat with her back against it for an hour, hoping Jack would come back.

But he didn't.

CHAPTER 8

"Oh, my fucking God," Hannah said in Carlotta's ear. "Are these photos what I think they are?"

Carlotta grimaced. "Yes." She glanced around the table where she sat in the hotel restaurant to make sure no one was within earshot. "It's the room where Patricia died. I took them last night. Sorry—I had to get them off my phone."

"You think her death wasn't an accident?"

"I don't know, but I want pictures of the scene just in case."

"Wait—are any of these dick pics of Jack?"

"No. Nothing happened with Jack. Those are spam prison porn."

"Phew. And send more when you can."

Carlotta shook her head, then ended the call. She looked up to see Jack stride into the restaurant, and waved to get his attention. She'd lain awake most of the night tossing and turning over why he'd come back to talk to her. Her eyes were so bloodshot, she was wearing sunglasses. He, on the other hand, looked fresh and full of vitality as he swung into the chair opposite her.

"Good morning!"

"Good morning," she murmured. "Sleep well?"

"Great," he said with a grin. "You?"

"Great," she parroted. "After you left, I took a long shower. It felt so good, I was in there for a while, like… forever. In fact, I missed two phone calls… couldn't hear a *thing*."

"Ah, too bad. Who called?"

"Hm?"

"The calls you missed—were they important?"

"Oh… it was Hannah."

"Both times?"

"Yeah, she... wanted to talk about Patricia."

"Ah, makes sense. No hotel owner wants a body count on their record. Sad business all the way around." He signaled the waiter for coffee, then looked back to her. "What's up with the sunglasses?"

"Just a little light sensitivity."

"Must be all the sunshine," he said happily.

"Must be."

He picked up the menu. "What looks good?"

"I might just stick with the coffee," she said. "I don't like to eat much before I fly."

The waiter brought a mug of coffee to the table. Jack waved off the cream and sugar, and ordered the Hungry Cowboy Platter.

"You're in a good mood," she observed.

He sipped his coffee, then nodded. "Yeah, I guess I am."

"Any particular reason?"

Jack shrugged his big shoulders. "I guess I needed a change of scenery to clear my head."

"Oh. Well, I'm glad. It was nice of you to come, Jack."

"I've enjoyed it. It was nice to have some downtime. The department is expanding and reorganizing, so when I get back to Atlanta, I don't think I'll have much time for leisure."

So she'd see even less of him than she did now. "How will the reorg affect you?"

He gave her a little smile. "I got a promotion, too."

She smiled in earnest. "That's great, Jack... congratulations."

His laugh was dry. "Thanks, but in law enforcement, a promotion usually means more stress and longer hours for the same pay." He made a thoughtful noise. "How will Patricia's death affect your workload?"

"Longer hours for sure, but—" She stopped and bit her tongue.

"But what?"

She sighed. "I don't want to speak ill of her."

"Was there a problem?"

"To be honest, it was a bit challenging to work with Patricia."

"Ms. Wren."

Carlotta looked up to see Detective Lawson standing next to the table, and from the look on her face, she'd heard that last comment. "Hello, Detective."

"We need to talk."

Her heartbeat sped up. Did they know she'd sneaked back into Patricia's room? Was she on camera?

Jack gave her a "what did you do?" glance, then said, "Have a seat, Detective. Coffee?" Without waiting for a response, he signaled the waiter to bring another cup.

Lawson sat down next to Jack, plopped a file folder labeled "Alexander, P" on the table, then leveled her gaze on Carlotta. "I don't mean to be rude, but I prefer to see the eyes of the person I'm questioning."

Carlotta removed the sunglasses and Jack's expression confirmed they were as bloodshot and sleep-deprived as she feared.

"Has there been a new development in the case?" Jack asked.

"You could say that," Lawson said. "We have a report from the airline that Ms. Alexander and Ms. Wren had an altercation on the plane."

Carlotta swallowed. "I wouldn't call it an altercation—it was a… disagreement."

The woman opened the folder. "According to the report, it was over a man?"

Carlotta held her up hands. "It's not the way it sounds. Patricia told me she was having dinner with the man she met online. I questioned if it was safe, and I suggested he might not be who he said he was considering the name he was using… and she took offense. She got a little loud, but I attributed that to the medication she was taking."

Lawson looked down to the report. "It also says something here about conflict on the job, that Ms. Alexander accused you of theft and insinuated you had received preferential treatment."

Carlotta squinted, trying to recall the conversation and how it could've been misconstrued. "Oh." Her cheeks warmed. "She was referring to a time earlier in my career when I abused my employee discount and return policy. I was penalized, and I paid back the company. My superior believes in giving people second chances, but I guess Patricia saw it as favoritism."

"So it's safe to say she thought you didn't deserve your position? That she resented working for you?"

"I don't think that was the case," Carlotta said. "Patricia was about to be let go, and I recommended her for the job as my assistant. She was appreciative."

Lawson looked back to the paper. "According to a woman who sat next to you, Ms. Alexander accused you of giving her the job as payback so you could order her around." Lawson narrowed her eyes. "Payback for what?"

Carlotta's throat constricted. She glanced at Jack, then back to Lawson. "Apparently, Patricia took the job with Neiman's in an arrangement with the D.A. to inform on me."

Jack's eyebrows climbed.

Lawson leaned in. "Inform on you for what?"

"If I may step in here," Jack said, "I can shed some light on that. Carlotta's father was a federal fugitive for a time. The D.A. was, shall we say, *overzealous*, in pursuit of leads, so it doesn't surprise me he planted someone at Carlotta's workplace. But Mr. Wren has since been exonerated."

"Patricia confessed on her own," Carlotta offered. "And she apologized. I decided to let bygones be bygones and offered her the job as my assistant."

"This report sounds a little overblown," Jack offered to the detective.

Lawson's mouth flattened. "Except the bartender of this restaurant came forward with an interesting story about Ms. Wren."

Carlotta's chest filled with dread. Where was this going?

"He said the two of you were flirting and made plans to hook up after his shift, but at some point you received a text from your coworker and you excused yourself to, quote, go take care of something. And when you returned a few minutes later, you had a bloody scratch on the back of your hand."

Jack's eyebrows were up again.

Carlotta's mind was spinning. "First of all, he was flirting alright, but we didn't make plans to hook up. The text I got from Patricia was the one I told you about—she said I was right about the John Smythe guy and she'd tell me about it later. I thought she needed cheering up, so I went to her room to try to convince her to come back to the bar with me."

"And what happened?"

"Nothing. She didn't answer the door, so I came back to the bar and had dinner."

"And did you hook up with the bartender?"

Carlotta flicked her gaze to Jack, who seemed equally curious. "No. I finished eating and went back to my room—alone."

"And how did you get that nasty scratch?" Lawson asked.

"I stuck my hand in my purse and snagged a sharp edge of my business card holder, that's all."

The woman picked up a napkin, dipped it in a glass of water on the table, then handed it to Carlotta. "Would you wipe off the makeup, please?"

Carlotta took the cloth and dabbed at the foundation she'd used to mask the cut, which had scabbed over. She winced at the pain as she reopened the wound and it began to bleed.

"Is this necessary?" Jack asked.

Lawson looked over. "You know it is, Detective." Then she asked Carlotta to place her hand on the table, and she photographed the abrasion.

"It's okay, Jack," Carlotta said. "I don't have anything to hide."

Except the fact that she'd gone back into Patricia's room to ransack for clues... which might lead them to believe she'd tweaked the evidence before she called the police.

Jack frowned, meaning he could tell she was lying.

Lawson set down her phone. "One might wonder if Ms. Alexander's phone is missing because the text messages between the two of you weren't as innocent as you say."

"Hold on—" Jack started.

"Here," Carlotta said, pulling out her phone. She went into her text app and sorted the messages by date. "I still have my texts from that night—you can read them yourself."

Lawson took the phone and tapped the screen a few times, then glanced up. "Are you into porn, Ms. Wren?"

Jack looked over her shoulder and his eyes went wide.

Carlotta flushed hot. "That's a spam issue from the Fulton County Correctional Facility." She looked at Jack. "I signed up to text with Peter."

"Oh, right, I heard about the breach."

"You're communicating with an inmate?" Lawson asked her.

Carlotta cleared her throat. "He's my ex-fiancé."

"Ah." Lawson looked back to the screen. "And who is Hannah?"

"She's a friend in Atlanta."

"You texted her about flirting with the bartender, I see."

Jack was still looking at her phone, too, and his expression suddenly changed. Carlotta tried to recall the gist of the text exchange with Hannah. *The bartender wants to shake and stir u?.... Yes, I don't think I should... Give me one reason and if u say Jack I'm going to have an aneurysm... What if I said Coop?*

Carlotta closed her eyes briefly and when she opened them, Jack gave her a little nod of acceptance.

"Hm," Lawson said.

"What?" Carlotta asked, alerted to the tone in her voice.

"Maybe you can explain this phrase from your friend. 'If you're gonna off her, do it in Texas.'"

Jack made a strangled noise.

Carlotta tried to laugh, but it came out sounding like she might throw up. "That's just my friend Hannah's dark sense of humor, right, Jack?"

"She can be dark," he agreed.

Carlotta sobered. "In hindsight, it was an unfortunate choice of words. If I were planning to harm Patricia, why would I text about it?"

"Because in my experience," Detective Lawson said, "criminals aren't that bright, and they think they won't get caught."

Carlotta gritted her teeth. "Did you find the texts between me and Patricia?"

Lawson nodded, and used her finger to scroll. Then she looked up. "And if we get the text transcripts from Ms. Alexander's phone, it will show the same conversation?"

"Absolutely," Carlotta said. "Plus the conversations she had with the online guy... and maybe the guy from the airport."

The female detective handed back her phone, then looked to Jack. "Detective, can you vouch for Ms. Wren?"

Jack took his sweet time responding, Carlotta noticed.

"Carlotta has an interesting history," he said, folding his hands on the table. "She has a motley collection of friends and relatives. And she's a meddling, irritating busybody."

Carlotta frowned.

"But I can vouch she didn't do anything to cause Ms. Alexander's death. In fact, Carlotta's interfering has kept a lot of people from being harmed, and even saved my butt a time or two."

Her heart warmed a little around the edges to hear his earnest defense of her. And it made her wonder all the more about what might've happened if she'd been in her room last night when he'd come back, instead of meddling in Patricia's case in the room across the hall.

Lawson's expression was stoic. "Okay, Ms. Wren, I'm going to take my colleague here at his word, and not detain you. Hopefully the autopsy will show Ms. Alexander's death was an accident, and this will all be a moot point. But if not... I'll be in touch."

Carlotta decided to let the woman have the last word. Jack stood and the detectives said their professional goodbyes.

When he sat back down, Carlotta wet her lips. "Jack—"

"Ah, good—breakfast," Jack said, moving his napkin so the waiter could set a giant plate of food in front of him. He picked up his silverware, then looked up. "You sure you don't want some of this?"

She nodded—she couldn't eat if she had to. "Jack... about the messages on my phone—"

"No need to explain," he said, cutting into a steak with gusto. "I was just happy to see there weren't any photos from the death scene."

Carlotta scoffed. "Of course not." Because she'd smartly sent them all to Hannah and deleted them.

She picked up her coffee cup and sipped while Jack put away pounds of meat and eggs. She would've given anything to know what he was thinking, and she longed to ask him why he'd come back to her door last night... if he'd planned to say the things he should've told her before, but hadn't?

But they had reached some kind of quiet impasse—she could feel the invisible wall between them.

And maybe it was for the best.

After breakfast they checked out of the hotel and headed to the airport. Carlotta watched the passing scenery in reverse, marveling at everything that had happened since she'd taken this route a couple of days before—with Patricia. Jack looked out the opposite window, seemingly in his own world.

When their ride-share car dropped them at the departures zone, Jack joined the line to check his bag at the curb.

"I'll be right back, Jack."

Before he could respond, she jogged across the pedestrian crosswalk to the taxi kiosk, looking for the man who had flirted with Patricia. But the man working the kiosk was a stranger.

"Excuse me?"

The man turned and smiled. "Yes?"

"I was looking for the man who was working here the day before yesterday—tall, brown hair?"

"That sounds like Trevor Biondi."

"I didn't get his name," she said.

"Ladies' man?"

She smiled. "Yes. He hit it off with my friend. Actually, I'm asking for her."

He made a rueful noise. "Tell her Trevor quit."

She frowned. "When?"

"Yesterday. He called in, said he was moving to the West Coast. Sorry."

"Thanks, anyway."

She hurried back to where Jack stood waiting. "What was all that about?"

"The guy Patricia gave her business card to quit yesterday. Doesn't that seem awfully coincidental?"

"In the service industry where turnover is sky-high? Not really." He grunted. "Leave it alone, Carlotta. I know you're upset about your friend, but making a murder out of a molehill isn't going to bring her back."

Carlotta pressed her lips together, then nodded. He was right... probably.

Jack offered to carry her roll-on to the gate. She let him because her hand was starting to throb from the reopened wound. They were studiously polite to each other, which left her chest tight with anguish. Why was everything always so out of sync?

Maybe you're the problem, Carlotta.

At the gate, they sat together but didn't talk. Jack seemed restless and distracted, as if he were tired of her company. That's how it would probably be if they were a couple, she thought, and all the better she hadn't answered the door last night to hear what he had to tell her. She excused herself to a smoking lounge and stood in a cloud of nicotine with a bunch of crusty old cowboys who were coughing and hacking as if they were taking their last breath. Her clothes would reek, she realized. She smoked only half a cigarette because she was wearing a patch and didn't want to overdo it. When she snubbed out the butt, she stared at it, then dropped it into a container full of sand. With newfound resolve, she removed the unfinished pack of cigarettes and tossed it, too.

At least something good would come out of this trip.

By the time she made it back to the gate, the flight was boarding. When she walked onto the plane, she recognized the flight attendant who had intervened between her and Patricia, and balked. He gave her a haughty stare—not totally undeserved, she admitted. But not nice, either.

When she and Jack were seated, he in the window seat and she on the aisle, her mind raced for a way to try to put things right between them. But he seemed fascinated by the in-flight magazine in the seat pocket, and by the entertainment choices on the small personal screens mounted in front of them. When the flight got underway, he plugged in earbuds to watch a movie for the two-hour flight.

Carlotta sat stock still, aching over unsaid things and ruminating on Patricia's senseless death. When the flight attendant came through with a refreshment cart, she requested a bottle of water. When he handed it to her, he asked, "Where's your friend?"

"She died," Carlotta said quietly.

His eyes widened, then he moved on.

Once, toward the end of the movie, she and Jack shifted at the same time, and their hands brushed on the armrest between them. She didn't pull away... and neither did he. He kept staring straight ahead, but his pinkie finger moved almost imperceptibly on top of hers. Considering how many times they'd had wild, jungle sex, the touch was more than chaste—it was downright virtuous. But the implied intimacy sent a jolt of awareness through her, and caused her to hope like she'd never hoped before.

But the contact ended in the flurry of preparing for descent into Atlanta. The landing was uneventful and they deplaned wordlessly. As they moved toward baggage claim to retrieve Jack's duffel, she couldn't help feeling that a door was closing on their time together. She hated the way she was missing him already.

Suddenly Jack came to a halt.

Carlotta's steps slowed. "Did you forget something?"

"No." He pulled his hand over his mouth. "I have to say something."

"O… kay."

"I went to Dallas because I thought it would be a good time and place to tell you something I should've told you long ago. I changed my mind when I got there—I guess I chickened out."

Carlotta's heart thudded against her breastbone.

"I know this isn't a good time or place to say it, but I can't keep it in any longer."

Anticipation rose in her chest, expanding her heart. This was it… this was what she'd been waiting for… "Go on, Jack."

He exhaled and appeared to be rallying for strength, then he lifted his gaze to hers. "Randolph isn't your biological father."

She froze, trying to process the words that weren't remotely similar to what she thought she would hear.

"Did you hear me? Randolph isn't your real father. I should've told you a long time ago."

Her mind swirled. "How…"

Then a memory emerged. Long ago, when someone who'd stolen her identity had died, she'd agreed to play along and have a mock funeral in case her fugitive father showed. While she was under wraps and under surveillance, Jack had stayed in the townhouse to keep an eye on things.

And without their permission, he'd secretly unwrapped, then rewrapped the Christmas gifts under the shabby little tree in the hopes Randolph had left some clue to his whereabouts.

He must've opened the locket and inferred from the picture and the note that, not knowing what the future held, Valerie had left Carlotta a life-altering message.

It explained why he kept asking if her family had held their postponed Christmas and unwrapped the gifts. Jack had known all this time.

Even worse... "That's what you were so tortured about telling me?"

He nodded. "Was I wrong? Are you okay?"

Jack wasn't in love with her... he never was, and never would be. She swallowed the lump of tears at the back of her throat. "My parents told me a couple of weeks ago." She pulled the pendant from her blouse and held up the locket.

His shoulders bowed in relief. "Good. You should've heard it from them. And are things okay?"

"Sure," she said breezily. "Things are just... peachy."

Jack angled his head. "Are you alright? Let me grab my bag and I'll drive you home."

"No, thanks," she said, pointing toward the Marta station. "I'll take the train. Bye, Jack. Thanks for coming to Dallas. You're a good... friend."

"Carlotta—"

She gave a little wave, then turned and marched in the opposite direction.

CHAPTER 9

WES'S FOREHEAD hit the counter with a *blam*! He jerked up and winced, then rubbed his sore head. He was going to have to start wearing a helmet to work the driving range counter.

He glanced at the clock and groaned. Nine hours left on his shift.

This was pure, unadulterated hell.

The counter phone rang and he picked it up. "Lindbergh Driving Range."

"It's your dad," Randolph said. "And it's Lindbergh *Family* Driving Range. When you answer the phone, you need to sound friendly. And don't forget to say our slogan, okay?"

"Okay, sorry."

"Has anyone answered the help wanted ad?"

"One guy, but he thought this was an indoor range. He passed."

Randolph emitted a frustrated noise. "Don't young people work anymore?"

"Kids would rather work at Six Flags or Lake Lanier Islands."

"Why don't you call that guy back and talk up the job a little?"

Wes rolled his eyes. "Okay." He so was not going to.

"I'm just thinking of you, son. The sooner you hire someone, the sooner you can delegate all the jobs around there you don't want to do."

Which would be—Wes counted in his head—all of them. "Got it. How's the move going?"

"Prissy has us all toeing the line. By the way, have you talked to Carlotta?"

"Yeah, she's back from her business trip early. There was a... thing with a coworker, they had to cancel the trip."

"Aw, too bad. Will you tell her I asked about her?"

"Yeah."

"Okay, I'll call you later."

"Later," Wes said, then hung up.

And exhaled.

He hoped this standoff between Carlotta and his parents was resolved soon... he hated being the go-between. More than anything, he hated to see Carlotta so unhappy. And the Dallas trip must have done her in because she seemed more withdrawn than ever.

The phone rang again, and he yanked it up. "Lindbergh Driving Range."

"Ha—caught you again," Randolph said. "Don't forget to say 'Family'."

"Right... sorry."

"And the slogan."

"Yep."

"Later, son."

Wes hung up the phone. "Fuck!"

He reached into his pocket, pulled out the little baggie of white Oxy pills and recounted them. They were all still there, had survived the freezing and the thawing. His tongue tingled, remembering the burn of the pills when he swallowed them, or better—when he chewed them. His visits with E. Jones would be done soon, and so would the threat of random drug testing. Then he could seek an escape from the unending monotony of this place.

He pushed the pills back into his pocket. Not that there wasn't plenty of work to do. Between dealing with customers, mowing the tees and the fairway, collecting balls from the fairway, then cleaning the balls and sorting them back into buckets, he stayed busy. But he was bored out of his mind.

His phone vibrated. He pulled it out, then grinned like an idiot to see a text from Meg.

Hi loverboy... On holiday with friends, biking thru Ireland. I got a new tattoo! They all say hi. Missing you some.

She'd sent a selfie showing off a tiny shoulder tattoo with a group of young people behind her, some of them off-camera. They all looked tanned and carefree and rich, like a commercial for one of those dipshit lifestyle brands.

Wes sighed. He wanted to be there.

He ran his finger over her smiling face. Her hair was blonder, her lips were pinker.

After a few attempts at a nonchalant reply, he wussed out and texted *Missing u too.*

Apparently, he was also missing his balls.

She sent back a little pink heart emoji, and he pursed his mouth. Last week she'd sent red heart emojis, and this week it was pink heart emojis... was she trying to tell him something? That her feelings for him were fading? Girls pulled that kind of secret-code bullshit to yank on guys' leashes.

He pulled up the selfie and scanned the faces of the people around her. The guy next to her with a man-bun grinned at the camera as if he had a secret. Wes realized he had his arm around Meg and was giving a thumbs up. Was that thumbs up, the hills in Ireland are great, bro? Or a thumbs up, I'm sharing a sleeping bag with your girlfriend?

He frowned and put hate on the guy anyway just for looking like a douchebag.

The bell on the door chimed, so Wes stowed his phone and donned his "Hello, asshole," smile. Then he grinned at the mismatched couple standing there. "Hey, Chance! Hannah!"

"Hey, dude."

"Hiya, Shithead."

He gave Chance a high five, then took a punch from Hannah. "Ow. What are you two old married folk doing here?"

Hannah held up a driver. "We came to give you some business. And it looks like we came just in time." She surveyed the shabby lobby. "This place sucks." She pointed toward the window. On the tee one old man stood bent over his club, frozen. "Is that guy dead?"

"He just takes a long time to wind up... and to swing."

"Jesus, how are you not blowing your brains out?" she asked.

"I don't have a gun."

"Okay, well, sell us a couple buckets of balls before this place turns into a horror movie."

Chance was walking around, sizing up everything, using the end of his driver to scratch his butt. He reeked of weed.

"Do you play golf, Hannah?" Wes asked.

"Yeah. My parents made me learn. Worst game ever, by the way."

"No, it's not," Chance said. "Golf is the closest game to the game we call life."

Wes and Hannah stared at him.

"The great Bobby Jones said that," he declared. "And it's fucking true."

"Okay, well, let's go hit some balls, Socrates."

Chance squinted. "Who?"

Hannah rolled her eyes, then picked up both buckets and carried them outside. Wes followed them out, giving them a nickel tour. "Over there's the bathhouse, with three johns. Over there's the base of an old fountain that used to be here."

"I remember that fountain," Chance said. "I used to drive by this place."

"What is your dad thinking?" Hannah asked, sticking a tee in the ground. "It's going to take a shit ton of work and shit ton of money to get this place back in the black."

Wes frowned. His dad was thinking it would be a cash business he could use as a tax shelter for Wes's poker playing, but so far, poker seemed way down on the list.

Hannah set down a ball, assumed a driving stance, pulled back, swung, and hit the ball with a sweet smack.

Wes stared open-mouthed as the ball arced high, and sailed past the two-hundred-fifty yard marker. "Holy shit, Hannah, that's almost three hundred yards." He knew nothing about golf and he knew that was remarkable.

"Yep," she said, then set and struck another ball that went just as far.

Two old-fart regulars who were making their way up to the shop stopped to gawk. Hannah struck quite a figure at nearly six feet, dressed in a black leather romper and combat boots. Her powerful arms and shoulders were covered in tattoos, and her body and face were pin-up stunning. She hit ball after ball with perfect form, sending them all to jaw-dropping yardage.

"Who is that?" one of the men asked in awe.

Wes was pretty sure the guy had a hard-on, probably his first in a decade.

"That's my wife," Chance said, thumping his chest, as if he were her muse.

By the time Hannah finished the second bucket of balls, she'd amassed a little audience of admirers. More than one person was shooting video of her. When she finished, the group applauded, and she took a bow.

"What's your name?" someone shouted, holding up their phones.

"I'm Hannah the Hammer, a roller derby girl!" she shouted. "I practice all the time here at—" She looked at Wes and whispered, "What's the name of this place?"

"Lindbergh Family Driving Range."

"At the Lindbergh Family Driving Range!" she crowed. "Everyone come out and join me!" Then she struck a pose and blew a kiss.

Wes grinned. "Post that to hashtag Where Winners are Made!" His dad would be so impressed.

"Hey, Dude," Chance said, pointing to the flyer on the window. "Are you hiring?"

Wes walked over. "Yeah. Do you know someone dumb enough to want to work at this godawful place?"

"Yeah—me."

Wes's eyes popped, then he stabbed at his glasses. "No shit?"

"No shit. I can do something with this place, man. And we'd have a blast!"

Wes surveyed his buddy Chance—slovenly, foul-mouthed, always high, and down a few million brain cells. His dad would positively loathe him.

"You're hired."

||||| |||||

CHAPTER 10

"Ms. Wren, this is Dr. Denton calling... again. I don't want to pester or annoy you, so if I'm doing either, please forgive me. I'm just reaching out."

Carlotta sighed, then deleted the voice mail message. The man was persistent, she'd give him that. But she was past thinking she needed a shrink. Lots of people had problems more serious than hers.

Look at Patricia, for example.

No, what she needed was a *drink*. With Hannah. At Moody's.

The Lyft driver pulled around and let her off in front of the cigar bar. She walked in and smiled at the lively atmosphere. Moody's was tucked into an original art deco building. The owner, June Moody, did her best to maintain her father's vision for the cigar store and smoking bar on the first floor, and the martini lounge on the second floor. It was a popular place for happy hour, although this evening it seemed more crowded than usual.

From behind the horseshoe-shaped bar, June waved, elegant as always in a starched white shirt with black piping trim. Carlotta waved back, then spotted Hannah at a high top, and made her way over.

"Hi."

"Hi, yourself." Hannah bit into her lip. "You look like shit. Do you still have the flu?"

"Uh, no. Just working really long hours at the store."

Hannah pushed a glass of brown liquor toward her. "I got you a bourbon, neat. Is everyone freaked out over Patricia?"

She nodded, then frowned. "And apparently the detective from Dallas called a few employees to ask if Patricia and I had 'issues.'"

"She's still implying you had something to do with it?"

Carlotta sighed. "Yes, and now everyone is looking at me like I'm some kind of psycho."

"That's not an insult. Not all psychos commit murder."

Carlotta looked at her.

"I'm just saying."

Carlotta sipped the bourbon and made a face, then swallowed. "The thing is, if I were Detective Lawson, I'd suspect me, too."

Hannah made a thoughtful noise. "And you can't blame your coworkers for being suspicious of you—there was that whole situation with Michael Lane who worked with you."

"Right."

"And the incident at the store when you were tracking the Charmed Killer."

"Uh-huh."

"And don't forget the Wedding Expo murders."

Carlotta frowned. "I get it. But I didn't commit those murders—I solved them."

"But nobody likes an overachiever," Hannah chided, wagging a black-tipped finger. "It looks fishy."

"I don't mind a little suspicion if it means Patricia's case will get the attention it deserves."

Hannah's mouth twitched down, then she lifted her glass. "To Patricia, who was a pain in the ass and an uptight little twit—"

"Hannah."

"—but we're really, truly sorry she's dead."

Carlotta clinked her glass to Hannah's. "Hear, hear." The second sip went down a little easier.

"When will the autopsy results be available?"

"I'm meeting Coop here, I was hoping he could pull a few strings to find out."

Hannah perked up. "Coop is coming?"

"Down, girl. You're a married woman."

"I didn't go blind when I married Chance."

Carlotta grinned. "Some think you went blind *before* you married him."

"Hardee har. He's a dumbass, but I love him. Wait—I think I just wrote a country-western song."

They laughed and took another drink of bourbon.

Carlotta propped her chin up with her hand. "How did you know?"

"How did I know what?"

"That you loved Chance?"

Hannah shrugged. "I didn't at first. He just wouldn't go away. And when I stopped to think about who would be there to hold my head over the toilet if I was puking out my guts, I thought, yeah, that's Chance. He's solid that way. And I fell for him."

Carlotta smiled. "That's really nice, Hannah. You figured it out."

"Thanks. You will, too. So what happened in Dallas with Jack?"

She shook her head. "There were some really nice moments, but ultimately, Jack is never going to commit to me, so I'm done with that."

Hannah guffawed. "You're such a liar, Carlotta."

Carlotta blinked. "I'm not a liar. I don't lie."

"Yes, you do. Every time you party crash and test drive a car for fun and sneak into prisons, you're lying. You even faked your own death!"

She frowned. "All of those things I did for good reasons."

"That's what most people tell themselves. Think about it—no one lies unless it's for a good reason."

"A good reason in their mind."

"Right. Like when I dress this way around my friends, and a different way around my family. It's a good lie."

"But a small lie by comparison."

"You mean in comparison to the lie I told about why I befriended you?"

Hannah's parents had been on the list of people who thought they were swindled by Randolph. "No." Carlotta took another sip of bourbon. "There are bigger lies than that."

"Like Liz's lie about the baby?"

"Well, yeah, although I think that wasn't so much a lie as a delusion."

Hannah pointed to the television over the bar where two potential presidential candidates were stumping. "What about lies public figures tell?"

"They're not all liars."

"Yes, they are. That's the point I'm trying to make. Everyone lies, just to different degrees."

Hadn't she said the very thing to Patricia to warn her about the man she'd met online?

That's what people do... they lie every day, all the time, every chance they get...

Except she'd been so patronizing. What if she had somehow instilled in Patricia a sense of paranoia that had triggered something to spoil the date... or to anger the man? She hadn't meant to project her insecurities onto the woman. Carlotta lifted a hand to rub her thumb over the locket she wore.

"That's cute," Hannah said, nodding to the pendant. "Is it new?"

She nodded. "Valerie gave it to me."

"Does it have pictures of your parents inside?"

"My father," she murmured. "When he was young."

"Can I see?"

"Um..."

But Hannah was suddenly distracted by someone past Carlotta's shoulder. She grinned and waved like a schoolgirl. "Hi, Coop!"

Carlotta turned to see the tall, handsome man striding toward them, hipster cool in dark jeans, slim-fit Henley t-shirt, and leather tennis shoes. His glasses were pewter colored metal. Her chest buoyed in admiration and affection. "Hi, Coop."

"Hi, Hannah. Hi, Carlotta." He threw a wave to June. "Wow, it's hopping in here tonight."

"I thought it was more crowded than usual, too," Carlotta said.

"Manchester's closed," he said. "That's where all the local attorneys and budding politicians hung out... looks like they migrated here."

"That explains why the TV's are playing C-Span instead of ESPN," Carlotta offered.

"Guess I'll have to watch soccer at home," he said.

"I *love* soccer," Hannah said, staring up at Coop. "I like to go studs up."

Coop smiled. "Studs up is an illegal maneuver, Hannah. You could get hurt."

"Exactly," she purred.

Carlotta kicked her under the table. "Coop, why don't you grab a chair?"

"You can have mine," Hannah groused. "As much as I'd love to stay, I gotta run. You kids have fun." She tossed back the last half-inch of bourbon, then marched out the door.

Coop smiled as he swung into the empty seat. "I didn't mean to run her off."

"You didn't. We were just catching up."

"Good to know I'm not the only person you haven't seen in a while."

"I've been working long hours at the store."

"Your father said you were under the weather."

"That, too," she murmured. "Then my Dallas trip went sideways."

"Yeah, I talked to Jack."

She lifted her glass for a drink. "Hm?"

"He told me about your coworker. Really sorry to hear it."

"Thanks. It was a shock." She shifted. "What did Jack have to say?"

"He said he flew down to smooth things over with the locals. Apparently they suspected you had something to do with it?"

"Yes... but that was all circumstantial."

"That's what Jack said. He asked me to take a look at the body when it arrives at the morgue."

She blinked in surprise. "Oh... good."

A waiter came by and Coop ordered a club soda. He pointed to Carlotta.

"I'll have another bourbon, neat."

"Rough day?" Coop asked.

"Rough year."

"You've been through a lot," he said, nodding.

"I'm sorry," they said in unison.

"For reacting like a fool—"

"For putting so much pressure on you—"

"—when Rainie told me about Liz's fake pregnancy."

"—when you were under so much strain."

They smiled.

"No worries."

"Nothing to apologize for."

She reached across the table to clasp his hand. "Tell me what's new with you."

"Same old, just working a lot. I try to find time to hike on the weekends, or take the 'Vette out for a drive."

Just the segue she was looking for. "Speaking of cars... I was wondering if you could give me some advice on selling the Miata."

His eyebrows climbed high. "You want to sell the convertible? I thought your dad got you that car."

"He did... when I was a teenager."

"But you kept it all this time."

"And now it's time for it to go," she said, a little more sharply than she meant. She cleared her throat. "I got a promotion at work, so I think it's high time I got a grownup vehicle."

"Congratulations," he said with a big smile. "Okay, sure. It's a great little car, low mileage, has been kept out of the elements. I'm sure collectors would be interested, but it would be worth a lot more if it were running."

"I got a quote from a repair shop a while ago, with a list of parts needed, but I couldn't afford it until now."

"I can swing by the townhome sometime when you're there and take a look at the list," he offered. "And take a look under the hood." His gaze swung down to her cleavage—accidental, or subconscious?

"That would be terrific. And I'm living back at the townhome with Wes, so I'm there when I'm not working."

"How is Wes?"

"He's working for Randolph at a driving range at Lindbergh, of all things."

Coop made a thoughtful noise. "I was hoping he'd go to school, but a family business is cool."

"Honestly, I think he hates it, but he doesn't know how to tell his dad."

"Your dad is a pretty intimidating guy," Coop offered.

She pressed her lips together, then nodded. "But Randolph is so impressed with you, Coop, for what you did for Mom. We all owe you such a debt."

"I was happy to help," he said. "But you know I did it for you, Carlotta."

Her bruised heart unfurled a little, and something occurred to her. "You've never lied to me, Coop."

He looked confused. "Why would I lie to you?"

Indeed. Coop was the guy who would hold her head over a toilet... he was solid... he was sexy... he was smart... but was he available?

"How's Rainie?" she asked.

"Rainie's great," he said, nodding. "She just got engaged to a dentist."

"Really?" She leaned toward him.

"Really." He leaned toward her. "And I couldn't be happier for her."

The waiter brought their drinks and Carlotta lifted her glass, locking gazes with Coop. "To Rainie being engaged."

Coop lifted his glass. "And to Jack being an idiot."

Carlotta smiled, then clinked her glass to his and drank deeply.

He held her gaze. "If we're going to do this, I want to do it right, take it nice and slow."

She nodded. Her mistake with Jack was jumping into bed with him early and often.

"Agreed. Nice... and slow."

CHAPTER 11

WALKING HOME from the train station, Carlotta sagged under the weight of another long day of countless decisions, emails, meetings, and phone calls. Her mind was mush, her eyes were scratchy, and her feet were not happy.

That said, she'd never experienced such a rush of satisfaction. She was good at this. And she looked forward to getting up in the morning and doing it again.

After a meal and a good night's sleep. And Wes, God love him, had texted her earlier that he was making a nice meal for them and not to be late. She was looking forward to catching up with him.

At the driveway leading to the townhome, she turned. When she spotted Mrs. Winningham near the fence, she tried to walk faster and more quietly, but Toofers saw her and set off the alarm, snarling as if she were a tall cat.

"Yoo hoo, Carlotta!" Mrs. Winningham called.

"Hello, Mrs. Winningham. I hope you're having a nice day." She kept walking, not intending to stop.

"It's much better now that workers aren't coming and going from your house, causing so much commotion."

"We hit the pause button on renovations for a while."

"Unfortunately, I've always had a perfect vantage point to your driveway. If you don't start being more considerate, I'll have to go back to keeping a log."

Carlotta stopped. "A log?"

The woman gave a curt nod. "When I realized the Wren family was going to be a problem, I started keeping a log of all the vehicles driving in and out at all hours of the day. That way when I called the police to complain, I had something to back it up."

Carlotta gave her a flat smile. "We'll try to be more considerate in the future. Have a good evening." She walked to the entrance of the townhome as fast as she could, dashing up the steps.

"Your yard needs to be fertilized!" the woman called. "And aerated!"

Carlotta leapt inside, then closed the door behind her. *Ugh.*

Then she smiled. The remodeled living room was tidy and the sound of Beth Hart floated out from the stereo system. A wonderful aroma wafted from the kitchen. She set down her purse and a stack of files to review later, then slipped off her shoes and followed the good smells.

The table was set for two. A bouquet of bright flowers in a vase was a nice touch.

Wes stood at the stove, stirring a pan of deliciousness.

"Something smells terrific," she said.

"Risotto," he said with a grin. "I burnt it to a crisp the last time I tried to make it for you."

"Thanks for trying again. The flowers are nice. Are we celebrating something?"

"Your promotion." He pointed to an uncorked bottle on the counter. "I'm using champagne."

Her chest brimmed with fuzzy warmth. "That's so sweet." She gave him a kiss on the cheek and he didn't even pull away.

"There's enough left to drink if you want. I bought two flutes, but they're plastic."

She smiled. "That's perfect." She filled up the two flutes with the pinkish bubbly. She sipped. "Mm."

"The guy at the liquor store said it was good," Wes said, sounding anxious.

"It is."

He tasted the risotto with a wooden spoon. "Are you ready to eat?"

"Yes. I'm starving."

"Have a seat."

She sat down at the table and let him fuss over her. She watched him, marveling how and when he'd stopped being a sweet, awkward boy and had turned onto a handsome, able man. He filled their plates with the thick, creamy risotto, then garnished it with basil leaves. From the refrigerator he removed a garden salad, and from the oven he withdrew a loaf of crusty bread.

"This is wonderful, Wes. Thank you."

He sat down, smiling. "You're welcome. Dig in."

She put a forkful of the risotto in her mouth, then moaned with pleasure. "This is so good. You're a magician."

He took a bite and seemed pleased with himself. "So, how is the new job? You sure are putting in a lot of hours."

"It's busy," she admitted. "But hopefully my schedule will ease up once the bridal salon opens. How's the golf business? You've been working long hours yourself."

He shrugged. "It's better since I hired Chance to help out."

"Hannah told me. How are Chance and Randolph getting along?"

"Dad doesn't know what to make of him yet."

She laughed. "I'll bet."

But at the mention of Randolph, they both fell quiet. She could feel Wes's eyes on her.

"Dad says hello. Mom, too."

She nodded. "Thanks."

Wesley set down his fork. "You have to talk to them sometime."

"I know. I'm just not ready."

"Does this change how you feel about me and Prissy?"

She looked up sharply. "No... of course not. You're my brother, and she's my sister, period."

"Then why does it change the way you feel about Mom and Dad?"

"It's not the same," she said. "They lied about it, kept it from me."

"Maybe your real dad was a bad guy."

She took a drink of the champagne. "I've thought of that."

"Or he could be dead."

"That, too."

"Do you want to know who he is?"

She shrugged. "I haven't decided. When I'm ready, I'll talk to Mom and Da—I mean, Randolph about it."

113

He looked worried.

"But I'll let you know," she added softly.

He nodded, then went back to eating.

"This is kind of like old times," she said to change the subject. She used her fork to indicate the two of them.

"Yeah, except now we can afford champagne."

She laughed. "True. And the kitchen looks great. The granite, and the new appliances. I can hardly remember what it looked like before."

"It looked bad," he said to remind her.

She laughed again. "Okay, I do remember. By the way, Mrs. Winningham is pissed about all the commotion over here."

He rolled his eyes. "She'd die if we weren't here to keep her stirred up."

"I think we should turn Prissy loose on her."

That made them both laugh. Carlotta felt a rush of affection for Wes and the good times they'd shared. No matter where life took them, she hoped they always remained close.

"So do you talk to Meg often?"

He chewed and nodded, then swallowed. "Every day she sends me a text or a picture or something."

"Do you miss her?"

"Yeah."

His tone was so heavy, her heart squeezed for him. "I'm sure she misses you, too. She'll be back soon."

But his expression made her think he wasn't so certain. "How about you? Who's the man of the hour?"

She tossed her napkin at him. "That's not nice."

"Now that Jack is off the hook from being Liz's baby-daddy, I figured he'd be coming back around with his big badass routine."

She shook her head. "No. That's... over."

In response, he took another drink of champagne. "Have you seen Coop lately?"

"We met at Moody's a couple of nights ago. He's going to come by and look at the Miata to see if he can get it running. I'm thinking about selling it."

That got a mild eyebrow raise, but he kept chewing.

"Coop asked about you. You're not going on body runs anymore?"

"Nah... that's a dead end job."

She laughed and he joined in, but she could tell he was joking to cover up his true feelings.

"I'm almost done with my community service," he said.

"That's great."

"Probably just in time to go to jail for the Vegas charges," he said dryly.

"Any news there?"

"Not yet. Dad said he'd find a lawyer who could take care of it."

"I'm sure he will," she soothed. "How's their move to the new house going?"

"I think they're almost done. Dad is not happy about that dog."

"Randolph would like to control the world," she offered quietly.

"He's good at a lot of things," Wes said.

"So are you. Don't forget that." She pushed back her plate. "Including this meal, ugh, I'm full. Thank you, again." She reached over and clasped his hand, then noticed his raw, red fingertips. She knew his habits—if he was biting his fingernails again, he was stressed. And she had a feeling Randolph was a big source of his anxiety.

He pulled his hand away to wipe his mouth with a napkin. "I have a surprise for you," he said, and he actually blushed.

Carlotta smiled. "What?"

He stood and jerked his thumb toward the living room. "I'll have to show you."

Her curiosity piqued, she stood up and followed him through the living room and down the hallway, past his bedroom and hers, to the end of the hall and the door to their parents' bedroom.

I wondered why this door was locked," she said. "What have you been up to?"

"This," he said, then pushed open the door.

Carlotta inhaled sharply. The dated, jampacked bedroom had been transformed into an elegant, beautiful office. The window frames and moldings were new, the walls were freshly painted white, and the dark hardwood from the rest of the house extended throughout the room. A black modern desk and matching bookcases dominated one side of the room. On the other side sat a red loveseat and two upholstered chairs around a glass coffee table. A large TV was mounted in the corner.

She covered her mouth with her hand. "This is for me?"

He nodded, then stabbed at his glasses. "I thought this would be better than working at the breakfast bar. Now that you're a director and all, you should have a home office."

Carlotta blinked back tears, but not fast enough.

"I did most of the work, and Mom helped to pick out the furniture. But if you don't like it—"

"I love it," she cried.

He grinned. "You do?"

She nodded, then pulled him in for a long squeeze. "You are the best brother I could ever ask for."

CHAPTER 12

TWENTY-TWO, TWENTY-THREE, twenty-four... Wes counted golf balls into buckets, tired as hell, and ready to get the eff out of there. *Twenty-five, twenty-six...*

The door to the lobby opened and Chance wrestled a huge container inside. "This is the last tub. I cleaned the johns and turned off the outside lights."

When he realized he'd lost count, Wes cursed, dumped the bucket, and started over. *One, two, three...*

"And the parking lot was looking kind of weedy, so I sprayed."

... eleven... twelve... thirteen...

"And I changed the oil in the mower. Man, that machine is awesome."

He lost count again. "Dude! I'm counting here."

"Sorry. My bad."

Wes was instantly contrite. Chance had been working his ass off, and incredibly, seemed happy as shit about it.

"Want some help?" Chance asked, jumping in. "I used to spend hours counting pills and putting them in little baggies. This is way easier."

Except Chance counted out loud, which threw Wes off again.

He stepped back, marveling over how much his buddy had taken to running the driving range. Chance seemed to be in his element, schmoozing with customers and running around the property finding ways to improve things. "Did you even smoke any weed today?"

Chance looked up. "No time. Do you want some now?"

Wes pursed his mouth, then shrugged. "Sure. We're done for the day."

Chance reached under his bill cap and pulled out a plastic baggie with a big fattie in it. He removed it reverently, then tucked the butt between his lips, pulled out a lighter and sucked on it like it was female until it caught. Then he inhaled deeply and held his breath, and passed it to Wes.

Wes took a deep draw, then coughed out most of the smoke. "Dude... this is strong. What is this stuff?"

"Banana Kush, man, it's some of the best grass ever. Don't waste it."

Wes tried again and managed to keep some of the smoke in his lungs. He instantly felt the high coming on. "Wow." He passed the joint back to Chance, who took another expert hit.

"I know, right? Yum. Never could understand why you liked that Oxy shit when you could have weed." He passed the joint back.

Wes inhaled. "You sold me that Oxy shit," he said while holding his breath. Then he passed the joint back.

"Well, I'm glad you're done with it."

Wes kept quiet, but the little bag of Oxy had burned into his leg all day. The only thing that had kept him from hitting it was being entertained by Chance. He took the joint for another hit, had just drawn a huge lungful when the door opened and Randolph walked in.

Wes coughed out a white cloud and stood frozen while his dad sized up the scene.

"What the hell is this?" Randolph demanded.

"Banana Kush," Chance supplied. "It's the most primo weed on the market right now, Mr. Wren. You want a hit?"

Wes closed his eyes briefly, praying to become invisible. But when he opened his eyes, he could still see himself, could see his hand holding the joint, shaking.

Randolph's face was mottled. "No, I don't want a hit. Put it out."

Wes used his fingers to pinch the fire at the end, wincing against the pain. Then he handed it back to Chance, who tucked it back into the baggie, and returned it under his cap.

"We had decent sales today," Chance offered, but the good news was somewhat mitigated by his slow, flabby delivery.

Randolph worked his mouth back and forth. "I can't believe you two. I'm trying to build a business here, and you're getting high?"

"We were just kicking back," Chance said.

"You are a bad influence on my son."

"Probably," Chance agreed with a shrug. "But Wes is a good influence on me. He used to take all my college exams, and got me real good grades."

Wes looked at Chance and shook his head.

"What? You were smarter than the professors who didn't even realize you weren't taking the class."

Randolph locked gazes with Wes, then pursed his mouth. "No smoking weed on the premises."

"Not even in the john?" Chance asked.

"Not even."

"How about while we're mowing? That shouldn't bother anyone."

Randolph put his hands on his hips. "Except it's probably not a good idea to operate heavy machinery while you're stoned."

"How about—"

"Dude," Wes cut in with a hiss. "Shut it." He hated that look of disappointment on his dad's face.

"You can't afford to get into any more trouble, young man."

"Did you just come back to lecture me?" Wes asked. The weed was making him brave.

"No. I came back because I bought you a chair in a poker tournament tonight in Peachtree City. Thought you could use some real-life practice."

Wes nodded. "Sure. Sounds good."

"Will you be able to play in two hours?"

"Yeah, I'll chug some Red Bull."

"Okay," Randolph said. "Let's go."

"Can I go, too?" Chance asked, sounding like an eager little kid.

Randolph hesitated, then nodded.

"Great!" Chance said, heading for the door. "Can we get some burgers on the way? Also I gotta warn you—smoking weed gives me gas, and whew, it will not be pleasant."

Randolph cut his gaze to Wes, who gave him a flat smile and followed Chance.

They piled into his dad's luxury SUV, and stopped to get takeout. Wes chowed down, hoping to soak up the high. True to his word, Chance passed enough wind to go airborne—they rolled down the windows and rode down I-75 south of the airport to Peachtree City, a town populated with lots of pilots, and lots of retirees.

The poker club was in the basement of a bar, and a typical tournament setup. There was a separate entrance for the players and the spectators so the management could keep a tight rein on the crowd. The buy-in was a grand. There were five tables, and five players at each table. The top player would take home ten grand, and the four other players at the final table would get back their buy-in money, plus a little extra.

Wes scanned the crowd, but he didn't see anyone he knew. He picked up his number then found the corresponding seat at a table. Three of the seats were occupied by men who seemed to know each other. They were chatting casually while each of them shuffled a deck of cards and went through their own warmup exercises. Randolph had given him a deck from the several he kept in his glove compartment, no doubt a holdover habit from when he dealt blackjack and poker in Vegas. Wes cut the deck and attempted a shuffle, but his tender fingertips nibbled down to the quick then burned by dousing the joint, made him awkward. He dropped the slick cards like a newbie, and glanced up to see if Randolph had noticed.

He had. His dad's mouth tightened in disapproval. Wes swallowed hard and tried to focus, but his left leg was jumping like mad. He glanced around the table to see if the other players had noticed. He realized the weed had made him a little paranoid.

Then the fifth player took their seat. He knew because he sensed a change in the rest of the players. Wes looked up to see a gorgeous Asian girl with a fall of white hair covering most of her face. She was wearing a thin white shirt and a red denim jacket with the collar turned up. She looked sullen and bored as she studied and seemed to dismiss each player.

Until she got to him. She leveled those black eyes on him and stared until he had to blink. She was mesmerizing.

The club manager announced the tournament's start, then a dealer joined each table and ran through the rules for Texas Hold 'em, how each player could use the community pot to improve their hand—a formality since everyone there knew the score.

Wes acknowledged a hum of excitement in his chest—he hadn't played cards since Vegas. He'd been on a winning streak until he was dragged out of the casino for playing with counterfeit bills.

But in Vegas Randolph hadn't been standing a few feet away watching every move.

He started off playing rocky, but thankfully two of the players were really terrible, probably on a married men's outing for the month while their wives did bookclub. They lost their thousand in chips pretty quickly, which left him and another guy and the foxy girl. She was so chill he might've thought she was tranquilized if not for the way her enormous eyes moved around the table and how confidently she bet.

Wes tried to play his game instead of hers, slow-playing good hands and bad hands alike. After four more rounds, the third guy was out, leaving him and Manga Girl to play for the table title. Randolph stood in his sight-line, arms crossed and judging.

Each of them had roughly half the chips the other three players had sacrificed. For the first six hands, they passed the lead back and forth. Wes was finding his zone, though, and on the seventh hand, he was dealt three of a kind, which improved to four of a kind with the turn of the community cards. He slow-played, as usual, and since she seemed to be willing to go along, he guessed she had a natural pair, and three of a kind with the community cards. He was contemplating his next raise when she removed her jacket.

She wasn't wearing a bra.

Talk about a natural pair.

Wes tried to avert his gaze, but it had been ages since he'd had sex. And there her nipples were, right there poking out in front of him. In the middle of the hand, he forgot what he was holding and had to look at his cards again. Oh, right—four of a kind. He went all in.

So did she.

The dealer pointed to him—he revealed his hand, and the spectators oohed. Then the dealer pointed to Manga Girl, and she turned over her cards.

"Straight flush," the dealer said. "We have a table winner!"

The crowd awed, then gave her a smattering of applause.

Wes stared, and the air left his lungs. He glanced up to Randolph, who wiped his hand over his mouth and turned away.

CHAPTER 13

CARLOTTA ZIPPED the white dress up the back until it caught. Contorting, she reached around and smoothed her fingernail over the teeth of the zipper, then eased the slider past the snag.

The drawback to wedding dress samples was they were tried on a lot.

She stepped back to view the dress in its entirety in the three-way mirror she'd purchased for her home office. Three large rolling racks held bagged dresses she'd sorted into "no," "yes," and "maybe." She was trying to choose which designer dresses would be showcased during the opening of the bridal salon. This Zac Posen embroidered halter gown was a definite maybe. The dress had a flared skirt that moved beautifully. And the touch of colored needlework flowers around the bodice was unique. Even better, it would pair prettily with a colored veil, which she planned to feature throughout the salon.

"Top of the news today," said the reporter on the TV mounted in the corner. "Officials in Arizona have arrested a man they say is the Red River Killer who eluded law enforcement for more than twenty years. Police worked with online ancestry databases to connect the DNA they had on file to this man. This could mark the beginning of a new and powerful tool for law enforcement to close cold cases in which they have DNA, but no suspect to compare it to."

"Amazing," Carlotta whispered to herself.

The chime of the doorbell sounded and she frowned. Probably another delivery from the store. She twisted to unzip the dress, but the zipper snagged again halfway down. She grunted in frustration, then decided the delivery person had surely seen more bizarre sights than a bride answering the door.

She lifted the skirt and walked barefoot out of her office, down the hallway, and through the living room to the front door. She peeked out the side window, then cringed.

Coop stood on the stoop.

But the man had seen her in worse getups, she reasoned.

She opened the door and his smile melted into surprise as he took in her full ensemble.

"Hi, Coop."

After he recovered, he gestured to his dress jeans and button-up shirt. "I feel underdressed."

She laughed. "I'm trying on samples for the salon opening. Come in."

He stepped inside. "I should've called, but I thought I'd take a chance you were here."

"I'm here."

He looked her up and down, then sighed. "Yes, you are."

Under his appreciative glance, her skin warmed. Coop was so handsome, and so... wonderful.

"Why did you stop by?"

"I can't remember," he murmured.

She grinned.

"Oh, right," he said, thumping his forehead. "The Miata. Still want me to take a look under the hood?" Except like the other night at Moody's, his gaze kept straying to *her* hood.

"If you have time," she said. "And if you brought your tools."

He wet his lips, then groaned. "I think I'd better go out to the garage before we violate our agreement. Is it unlocked?"

She nodded. "I'll change and come out." Then she turned. "But my zipper is stuck... can you help me?"

He came up behind her and lowered his mouth to her ear. "You're killing me."

His tongue darted out to skate along the column of her neck. Her nipples budded against the silky lining of the dress. She moaned.

His hand moved to her zipper, then he lowered it... trailing his fingers down her back as it opened inch by inch.

"Mm," she murmured. "We're going to have to... set some... guidelines."

"Uh-huh. Like me not being in a room alone with you when you're half-naked."

She stepped back into him, relishing the brush of his shirt on her bare back. He curled an arm under her breasts and pulled her against him. At the curve of her hip, she could feel a hardness...

Then it vibrated, and a ring sounded. His phone clipped to his waist, she realized.

Coop groaned in frustration. "Damn, I'm on call... I have to see who this is."

"Okay," she said with a little laugh. She turned around, holding the dress together.

Coop unclipped his phone, then sighed. "You've got to be kidding me." He pressed a button, then put the phone up to his ear. "Hi, Jack... what's up?"

Carlotta winced inside.

"Yeah," Coop said. "I took a look at the toxicology report on the Alexander woman, like you asked." He glanced at Carlotta to include her. "She did have alprazolam—Xanax—in her system, but not an excessive amount. And I agree with the findings on the autopsy—skull fracture that resulted in traumatic brain injury, but as to what caused it, I can't say. Could she have passed out and hit her head that hard? Sure."

"Was the hyoid bone intact?" Carlotta asked.

Coop gave her a flat smile, then said, "Yep, that's Carlotta. Why don't I put you on speaker so we can all talk about it?" He held out his phone, then tapped the screen. "You there, Jack?"

"I'm here," Jack said.

"Hi, Jack," Carlota said.

"Hello. What are you two into?"

"Uh..."

"Um..."

"Never mind," Jack said. "Coop, you were about to answer Carlotta's question about the hyoid?"

"Right," Coop said. "The hyoid bone was intact—she wasn't strangled."

"But could someone have pushed her down?" Carlotta asked.

"It's possible," Coop said.

"Or someone could've held her down?" Jack asked. "Hit her head against the floor?"

"That's possible, too," Coop said. "Although normally when someone else causes the head to hit the floor, the fracture is more severe."

"What about the marks Carlotta said she saw on the neck?" Jack asked.

"I did see them," she said irritably.

"I saw the marks, too," Coop said. "But they weren't identifiable." He gave her an apologetic glance.

"Okay, anything else?" Jack asked.

"I don't think so," Carlotta said.

"I was talking to Coop, the actual expert."

Coop laughed, and Carlotta made a face.

"No," Coop said. "I didn't see anything else that stood out."

"Thanks, Coop. Carlotta, I'll let you know when I hear from Detective Lawson about the outcome of the investigation."

"Okay, Jack."

"Sorry to interrupt."

A click indicated he'd left the call. "I'm not sure he is sorry," Coop said wryly, then stowed his phone. "But I'm glad you got to hear all that."

She nodded. "So you think Patricia's death was just an accident?"

"What I think doesn't matter. In the absence of forensic evidence or an eye witness report or a confession indicating foul play, the death is ruled accidental." He reached for her. "Now... where were we?"

She looped her arms around his neck and kissed him, a really nice, hot kiss. His hands started to slide down her bare back, then he groaned and lifted his arms. "No... we promised each other we'd take things slow, so I'm going out to the garage while you change out of that wedding gown."

She laughed and pushed him toward the door while she headed back to her office to change. Happiness bubbled up in her chest. She loved this playful side of sex, the buildup, the getting to know each other. It was the part most couples bypassed these days on the road to jumping into bed before they even knew if they liked the other person.

It was the part she'd bypassed with Jack.

Carlotta hastily changed out of the gown and into a skirt and blouse, and pushed her feet into sandals. Then she stopped by the kitchen to grab two bottles of flavored water and carried them outside. As she descended the steps, she glanced over to see Mrs. Winningham copying down information about Coop's van— Property of the Fulton County Morgue—in a notebook.

"Hello, Mrs. Winningham."

"Is there a dead body in that van?" she demanded.

"Probably," Carlotta lied. "Have a good day!"

She smiled to herself and walked to the two-car garage. Coop had lifted the rolling door and was standing at the front of the white Miata convertible, peering under the hood. As always, when she saw the car, she was flooded with nostalgia. It had been her first car, Randolph had given it to her along with a special keyring. She had loved it, had loved being the envy of every girl in her high school when she drove it.

Then her parents had left and the gift had seemed bittersweet, especially when it broke down and she couldn't afford to fix it. Except for the one otherworldly trip she'd taken in it once when she was under the influence of too many painkillers, it had sat here in the garage for—she counted—ten years?

When they desperately needed the money, she hadn't been able to part with it. But now just looking at the compact convertible was a reminder that everything she'd shared with Randolph had been based on a lie.

Coop smiled as she walked up, and took the bottle of water she offered.

"I see you found my repair estimate," she said, nodding to the faded form he held. "Is it still relevant?"

"Yeah, I think so, give or take a few minor parts." He winced. "And the tires are dry-rotted, as expected. But overall, I don't see any reason I couldn't get it running again."

"You?" she asked.

He shrugged. "I'd enjoy working on it, unless you're in a rush to get rid of it to buy a new car."

She wet her lips. "Not a big rush, no. I take the train almost everywhere."

"And I wouldn't mind having a reason to come over and hang out."

"You don't need a reason."

He grinned. "But I'll need something to keep my hands busy while I'm here."

Carlotta laughed. "Okay, sure. As long as you let me buy the parts."

"I'll start rounding them up." He lowered the hood, then took a drink of the bottled water.

"Did you happen to see the news today?" she asked casually.

"Not really. What did I miss?"

"There was a report that police tracked down a serial killer by sending his DNA to an ancestry site. How does that work?"

Coop pursed his mouth. "When people buy a DNA kit and send off a sample, they usually do it with the thought of tracing their family tree. The companies that offer the tests have been able to record and link millions of people through their networks. In this case, it sounds as if the police submitted the DNA for their suspect and it was linked to relatives who were already in the database. The closer the relative that was matched, the less work the police had to do."

Her mind raced to figure out if what she had in mind was even possible. "So if you submit a DNA sample, the company will know who you are and where you live?"

"Unless you submit a sample under a fake name... I guess that could be done, maybe?" Then he shrugged. "But why would someone do that?" His phone vibrated. Coop pulled it out, then winced. "Gotta run. I'll call you."

She nodded, then lifted her mouth for a goodbye kiss. Carlotta waved as he drove away, her mind churning. Why would someone do that, indeed.

‖‖ ‖‖

CHAPTER 14

"WE'RE GONNA miss you around here," Jeff Spooner said to Wes. He extended his arm as if to include the entire department of ASS, even though no else was looking up from their screen. And everyone wore headphones.

"Yeah," parroted Ravi Chopra. "Who's going to make fun of us?"

"Meg will pick up the slack when she comes back," Wes said.

Ravi leaned closer. "I'll bet she's a good kisser, isn't she?"

Wes slapped the poor guy on the back. "Yes. Yes, she is."

"We're all going to be working for her someday, aren't we?" Jeff asked.

"Probably," Wes agreed.

"Will you tell her we said hello the next time you talk to her?" Ravi asked.

"I sure will. You guys take care, and take a shower once in a while, okay?"

"Okay," they chorused.

Wes waved and walked away from the fourplex work station they'd shared, nursing a pang of sympathy for the lovesick losers.

Then he sighed. It took one to know one.

He hadn't heard from Meg yesterday, and it was already late in the day in her part of the world. But truthfully, he almost didn't want to hear from her because he was sure she was going to break up with him. She was probably boinking the man-bun guy and hanging out on topless beaches and showing off her new tattoo. And thinking about her loser boyfriend who'd never left the United States.

He stopped by his boss's office to say goodbye. Richard McCormick was a slouchy, middle-aged geek, but he was a standup guy.

As Wes left the building, he realized he was going to miss this place that had become such a pain in his ass. If not for his community service sentence, he would've never met Meg. He'd hoped they'd be telling that cute-meet story to their kids someday.

He sighed. But since he would probably never have sex again, kids didn't seem to be in his future.

He was unlocking his bike when he heard a horn sound. For a second he hoped Mouse had swung by in the big black Town Car with a bag of burgers. But when he turned around, it was Randolph's SUV sitting at the curb. The window zoomed down and his dad waved. "Get in. Put your bike in the back."

Wes walked his bike over, lifted the hatch, and stowed his bike in the cargo space. Then he walked around and climbed into the passenger seat.

"Hi," Randolph said, then nodded to the console. "I brought you some coffee."

Bitter and black, no doubt, but Wes nodded his thanks. "How did you know I was here?"

Randolph pulled into traffic. "I used a phone finder app."

Wes pushed his tongue into his cheek. A hazard of having his phone on his Dad's family plan.

"Bet you're glad to be done with that place," Randolph said, nodding to the shabby city building.

"Yeah," Wes said, then felt compelled to add, "But it wasn't all bad."

"That's where you met your girlfriend, isn't it?"

"Yeah. Meg's her name."

"Right, Meg. She's cute. You're using protection, right?"

Wes squirmed. "She's on the Pill."

"Still… you can't take any chances."

Wes wanted to point out that he should be so lucky to have a kid with Meg, but decided against it. "She's in Europe for the summer."

Randolph made a rueful noise. "Good thing she's on the Pill."

Wes gritted his teeth and looked away. "Thanks for the ride to the range, but you didn't have to. Chance was going to pick me up."

"Actually, I wanted to let you know I found you an attorney who's going to tackle the Vegas charges."

"Does he think he can get me off?"

"For the money I paid, I certainly hope so."

Wes chewed on his tongue to keep from pointing out his charges in Vegas all stemmed from Randolph—if he hadn't found the counterfeit money in the wall, he wouldn't have gone on a gambling junket. And he wouldn't have needed a fake ID. And it was his fuckup that had busted the whole Mashburn & Tully scheme wide open.

"What's the attorney's name?"

"I'll get you his card," Randolph said dismissively. "Birch is working with him directly."

Wes squinted. "What's his deal anyway?"

"Who?"

"Birch. Is he your secretary or Mom's nurse or Prissy's babysitter or what?"

Randolph shrugged. "I guess you could say he's our family helper."

That wasn't vague at all.

"How's Carlotta?"

Wes turned his head to look out the window. "She's busy with her job, but she seems okay. We talked the other night about... what happened with the Christmas gifts."

"She's still angry, I'm sure."

"She'll come around," Wes said. "She just needs some time."

"Do you know if she's been to see Peter lately?"

He didn't like being treated as an informant, although the question seemed innocent enough. "It hasn't come up. But I don't think she's carrying a torch for him anymore, if that's what you're worried about."

"That Detective Terry seems to hang around her a lot."

Wes laughed. "Yeah. She says that's over, but I doubt it." He swallowed. "I always kind of hoped she and Coop would wind up together."

Randolph pursed his mouth and nodded. "Coop's a good guy. I will never forget what he did for your mother. But he's a recovering alcoholic, and I don't trust addicts."

Wes bit down hard on his tongue. The little bag of Oxy pills was in his backpack, had been singing to him all morning.

Randolph shifted in his seat. "So I've been thinking."

Shit. "About what?"

"About your abysmal performance at the poker tournament the other night."

"That girl beat me with a straight flush—that's impossible."

"That girl beat you because she broke your concentration. If you'd handled the bids correctly, you would've known she had a hand that could top yours."

Wes frowned. Not untrue.

Randolph gave his turn signal, then pulled into a parking lot of a night club. Since it was the middle of the day, the place was quiet. His dad opened the door and climbed out, so Wes did the same.

"What's this?" he asked.

"I've decided you need a coach."

"A card coach?"

"Right. Someone to get you up to speed more quickly, someone who's played at the level where we want you to be."

Wes noticed the "we" reference, but let it slide. He followed his dad through a side door and into a darkened bar. It was quiet, except for the ruffling sound of cards being shuffled. When they turned the corner, Wes came up short.

The sexy gorgeous Asian girl sat at a round table behind a stack of cards and a stack of chips.

"Wes, you remember Jade."

She looked up, leveled those enormous eyes on him, then indicated the chair across from her. "Sit. Let's get started."

CHAPTER 15

AT THE RAP on her door, Carlotta looked up to see Lindy sticking her head inside. "Would you like to ride with me to the memorial service?"

Carlotta smiled. "I was going to take the train to the church, but sure, that would be nice." She picked up her bag, then fell in step with her boss. "This is such a sad day."

"Yes... especially for Patricia's parents, I'm sure. Do you know them?"

She averted her gaze. "Not really, no. I believe our parents might have socialized years ago." Hess and Laura Alexander had been clients of Randolph's and lost everything in the scandal that unfolded before he'd skipped town. Patricia had reason to resent the Wrens... Carlotta didn't blame her for agreeing to spy on her for the D.A.

"Before I forget to mention it," Lindy said, "I had a chance to review the gowns you chose for the opening showcase of the salon—very nice. And featuring colored veils... that's the kind of thing that will get us a mention in *Vogue*'s bridal guide."

Carlotta beamed under the praise. "I'm glad you approve."

They walked outside to the mall valet stand and Lindy presented her ticket.

"Also... I don't mean to sound crass, especially considering the somber occasion, but have you found any promising candidates to be your assistant?"

Carlotta sighed. "Let's see—there was the woman who wanted a one-month advance on her salary, the guy who only works on Tuesdays, and the woman who got up and literally ran out of my office when I said I'd be contacting her former employers."

Lindy cringed. Her luxury sedan appeared, and they climbed in.

Carlotta closed the passenger door and fastened her seatbelt. "There are a couple of applicants who appear reliable... but they don't seem to have a love for fashion."

"Fashion is in your blood, Carlotta. Not everyone has the eye you have."

The phrase "in your blood" suddenly struck her as odd. She'd never thought about it before, that society attributes much of what a person is to traits and characteristics inherited.

But then again, she'd never before had to think about where her blood had come from. She looked like Valerie, which she realized had made it easier to maintain the secret of her parentage... but she was fifty percent someone she knew nothing about.

The drive to the church was brief, and Carlotta was gratified to see the parking lot was nearly full. Patricia would be so pleased.

They filed into the church just as organ music started to play and found a seat in a rear pew. The sanctuary was simple, but elegant, with stained-glass windows depicting uplifting scenes of angels and celestial love. Carlotta wasn't a fan of organized religion, but she understood the comfort people drew from religious rituals like funerals and weddings and christenings. She drew comfort from them as well.

The rear seat gave her an opportunity to peruse the crowd. She saw many familiar faces from Neiman's, and she was pleased to see Patricia's former fiancé Leo, who played for the Atlanta Braves farm team. Carlotta wondered if the man harbored regrets, and it made her think about what the men around her might regret if her life was suddenly cut short.

Would Peter regret abandoning her when her parents had fled?

Would Jack regret not revealing more of himself to her?

Would Coop regret their pledge to take their relationship nice and slow?

A tall figure sidled into their pew. Carlotta smiled to see Hannah, dressed head to toe in black Halston that covered her tattoos, her hair demurely tamed in a low bun, and minus the face jewelry. She made room for her friend to wedge in.

"Nice of you to come," Carlotta whispered.

"Don't tell anyone I'm a nice person," Hannah whispered back.

Carlotta smothered a smile, then her gaze stopped on a couple sitting on the other side of the church—Randolph and Valerie. A wave of betrayal washed over her, and sudden tears welled in her eyes.

Hannah pushed a tissue into her hand, mistaking her tears for mourning, she was sure. Carlotta gave herself a mental shake, then turned her attention to the ceremony. A picture of Patricia, smiling, sat on an easel next to a closed coffin. Carlotta focused on the photo of live Patricia so she didn't think about the image of dead Patricia, lying face up on a cold bathroom floor, in a halo of her own blood.

The eulogy was brief and somber. The minister gave a short sermon on living life as if it could end at any moment. But the most heartrending part was when Patricia's father stood to address the audience.

"To most of you, Patricia was a friend or a schoolmate or a colleague. But to me she will always be my precious little girl who loved clothes and makeup and all things feminine and pretty. She always had a kiss and a hug for me, her dotty old dad. I couldn't have asked for a better daughter." His voice broke at the end, and everyone was visibly moved. Carlotta shot a look toward her parents and found Randolph looking back at her, his eyes sorrowful. They maintained eye contact until the minister asked everyone to stand.

When the service was dismissed, Carlotta turned to Lindy. "I'll find a way back to the office."

Lindy nodded, then joined the exiting mourners.

"Whew, that was rough," Hannah said, wiping at tearstains. "I guess you don't know how much your parents care until you have your own kids." She blew her nose loudly. "Well, not my real mom because she didn't care about anyone but herself. But my stepmom would be devastated if anything happened to one of us."

Carlotta was listening, but she was looking for Randolph and Valerie. "Can I get a ride back to the store?"

"Sure."

"Okay, give me a few minutes."

"I'm in the Audi, just come find me when you're ready."

Carlotta threaded through the crowd, then spotted her parents in the stream of people heading for the side exit. She caught up to them and touched her mother's arm. Valerie turned around, then her face erupted in a smile. "Hello, dear."

"Hi, Mom." Then she looked to Randolph. "Dad."

He smiled and leaned in to give her a kiss. "We're sorry to hear about your friend. You must've been in Dallas with her when it happened."

Carlotta nodded. "I was."

"Wes told us your trip was cancelled," Valerie said, "but we didn't connect the dots until we talked to Hess and Laura. They're inconsolable, of course. Losing a daughter—" Valerie cut off and dabbed at her moist eyes.

Carlotta stepped aside to let others go by them. "Can we talk for a minute?"

"Sure."

"Of course, dear."

They walked a few feet away to a quiet area of the church. Valerie's face was pinched and Randolph looked anxious as well.

Carlotta inhaled. "I love you both. And it's going to take some time for me to adjust. But I've decided I don't want to know who my biological father is."

Valerie's body sagged with relief, and Randolph's eyes glistened with unshed tears. Her mother embraced her, squeezing hard. "Thank you, darling. And please forgive me," she whispered. "I just want this all buried and forgotten. Randolph's name is on your birth certificate. He's your father by virtue of choice, which is a higher love."

Carlotta pulled back and wiped at her eyes, then went into her father's strong arms.

"I love you, sweetheart," he whispered.

She hugged him hard, remembering all the times she'd wanted to touch him during the years he was gone and couldn't. When they parted, they were both smiling.

"I have to go," Carlotta said, "but I'll come by soon."

They said their goodbyes, then she hurried toward the parking lot, trying to compose herself before she had to face Hannah. Like Valerie, she wanted the notion of her biological father buried and forgotten.

But despite her words, she wasn't quite there yet.

CHAPTER 16

"Hurry and pick your assistant," Prissy said, "so we can go shopping." She sighed dramatically. "How hard could it be?"

Carlotta gave a little laugh as she compared the two lackluster applications she'd narrowed the choice down to. "You have no idea."

Prissy walked around her cramped Neiman's office, peering into boxes and poking bags. "I like your office at the townhouse much better."

"So do I."

"I could be your assistant someday."

Carlotta smiled at her little sister. "I'd like that, except I have a feeling you'd need to be the boss."

Prissy grinned. "Daddy says you and I are both bossy girls. I'm glad we're alike."

Carlotta's heart swelled. "Me too."

"When is Mr. Jack coming to see me?"

"Soon," she murmured. "He's very busy."

"Is he busy with the baby he's having with that bad woman?"

Carlotta looked up, then shook her head. "No. There is no baby. The bad woman lied."

"That's a terrible lie."

Carlotta nodded. "Yes, the worst kind."

Prissy angled her head. "Do you ever lie?"

Ugh, the girl knew how to go for the jugular.

"Everyone lies," she said carefully. "Sometimes we tell lies to protect other people's feelings."

"Like when I told Amanda Gibson I liked her tennis shoes, when I really thought they were completely inappropriate with her sundress?"

Carlotta laughed. "Something like that. But just remember when you lie to someone, you're not letting them see the real you."

Prissy thought about it, then nodded. "Okay." Then she made a pouty face. "Can we go shopping already?"

"Okay," Carlotta said with a sigh, looking back and forth between the two resumes. "I'm just going to choose with eenie meenie miney moe."

A knock sounded on her door. She glanced up to see a smartly dressed man smiling at her.

"May I help you?" she asked.

"Carlotta Wren." He grinned to reveal the most perfect teeth she'd ever seen.

A memory chord stirred. "I know you."

"I'm Quinten Gallagher. I used to be—"

"The receptionist at Mashburn & Tully," she finished. "I remember." And she remembered how much she'd liked the man. "How are you?"

"Unemployed," he said brightly. "Like everyone else at that vortex of corruption. Which is why I'm here. I understand you're looking for an assistant."

She set aside the two applications she'd been reviewing. "I am. Someone to help me launch the new bridal salon."

"Hire me," he said. "I'd be a great assistant. And since I'm a pariah with Mashburn & Tully on my resume, no one else seems to want me. You're one of the few people who understand everyone who worked there wasn't to blame for what happened."

"I do know," she murmured.

"Besides," he said, "I always liked you and I think we'd work well together."

Carlotta sat forward. "I always liked you, too."

"So?"

She stood and extended her hand. "Okay. I'll let my boss know and HR will call you with the offer."

"Terrific." He shook her hand with enthusiasm, then he looked at Prissy. "And who's this little lookalike?"

"I'm Priscilla Wren. I'm Carlotta's sister."

"I can tell you're family for sure. I hope to see you again soon, Prissy. Thank you, Carlotta."

"No—thank *you*," she said. "You just made my day."

He left and she chucked the two applications in the trashcan.

"Can we go now?" Prissy whined.

"Yes," Carlotta said, reaching for her purse. "How much is this pool party ensemble going to cost me?"

"Probably a lot," Priscilla said earnestly.

She laughed and followed Prissy to the children's department. Within a few minutes, the girl had chosen a dozen dresses and bathing suits to try on. Carlotta settled into a chair in the sitting area of the dressing room and tried to empty her mind. It was impossible not to be happy with her family when she was with Prissy.

But it was getting harder and harder to quiet the yearning rising in her. Someone—Hannah, June?—had once commented that the reason she bounced back and forth between three vastly different love interests was because she was in a constant search for a reliable man in her life. She thought that search would come to an end when Randolph returned. Yet as much as she'd adored him, she had unresolved resentment toward him… and it was hard to put all her fatherly love in one place when she knew the possibility of another option existed.

Her phone rang. When she pulled it out, she frowned at the sight of the number she'd memorized by now—Dr. Denton. Deciding to put an end to his calling, she answered.

"Dr. Denton, I've received all your voice mails. Please don't call anymore."

"This will be my last call," he said. "I just wanted to speak to you voice to voice to say how deeply sorry I am for the incident with George. He's a kind, but troubled person. I wanted to assure you that you have nothing to fear from him." He made a thoughtful noise. "I don't expect you to understand this, but he spends a great deal of his time pretending to be someone else. Most of his capers and made-up personalities are harmless, but this time he went too far. I'm working with him to help him understand how his lies can harm other people. I hope you will find it in your heart to forgive him."

Carlotta swallowed hard. How many disguises had she donned in recent years to talk her way into places she didn't belong, or to elude being recognized? "Actually, you might be surprised how much I understand the desire to be someone else."

"Thank you for that," he said. "And for not hanging up. I wish you well, Ms. Wren, and I hope you've found someone to talk to about whatever drove you to seek me out in the first place."

She pressed her lips together. "Dr. Denton?"

"Yes?"

"I'd like to make another appointment."

CHAPTER 17

"DUDE, ARE you trying to burn this place down?" Chance asked.

Wes lowered his bloody fingers from his mouth and looked up. "Hm?"

"The coffee pot," Chance said, pushing it from the burner. "The handle is melted."

The scent of scorched coffee and plastic rode the air.

Wes straightened. "Uh, sorry. I didn't notice."

"What is with you today, man? Thinking about that foxy card coach of yours?"

"No," he mumbled. Although he should be. He hadn't heard from Meg in days and she wasn't returning his texts. If she was done with him, he had every right to be jerking off to the mental picture of Jade, braless.

"What then?" Chance looked him over. "Are you doing Oxy again?"

"No," Wes snapped. "I don't need you busting my balls, too."

Chance lifted his hands. "Okay, okay. If anyone wants me, I'll be dropping a deuce in the john."

He left, and Wes winced. His buddy meant well. He was the one overreacting.

The door chimed and Wes tamped down the annoyance of dealing with another customer—an irritating side effect of the uptick in business.

"Hiya, Little Man, what's shakin'?"

Wes turned and grinned. "Mouse! How's it going?"

The big man walked closer. "Good, no complaints."

"You come to hit a bucket of balls?"

"Nah, I can't today." He lifted a bag. "I brought you something."

"What is it?"

Mouse tossed it to him. "Here, open it."

The bag was heavy. He set it on the counter, then pulled out two books, *Study Guide for the ACT College Entrance Exam* and *Study Guide for the SAT College Entrance Exam.*

"I didn't know which one you'd need, so I got both."

Sissy tears welled in his eyes. He cleared his throat. "Thanks, man. This is so nice."

The door opened and Randolph walked in, glaring at Mouse. "You again. Did you come to do another hatchet job on my tee?"

"Nah... I brought Wes a present."

Randolph took a step forward to scan the titles of the books. His mouth turned down. "That was nice of you, but Wes isn't going to go to college."

"Maybe he'll change his mind," Mouse said. "You never know."

A muscle ticked in Randolph's jaw. "Look, friend. I appreciate you looking out for my son when I wasn't able to be with him, but I'm back now. Wes and I will decide what's right for his future."

Mouse pursed his mouth. "Actually, that's Wes's decision, not mine and not yours."

"Wes," Randolph said evenly, "we have an appointment with your poker coach. Tell your friend he should go."

Wes bit down hard on his cheek.

"It's okay, Wes. I'm going. See you later." Mouse turned around and lumbered to the door, then walked out.

Wes scowled at Randolph, who turned in the opposite direction and exited to the range tee where he instantly put on a smile for two customers slogging away at their balls.

Wes took off after Mouse and caught up to him in the parking lot. "Mouse!"

The big man turned around. "I didn't mean to cause trouble between you and your dad."

"It's okay. Thanks for the books." He lunged forward and gave the man a two-second hug.

"You're welcome," Mouse said with a big goofy smile, then swung into his car. "I hope you use 'em someday." He closed the door and turned over the engine.

Wes walked over and knocked on the window.

It buzzed down. "Yeah?" Mouse said.

"I need to give you something."

"Okay."

Wes dug into his pocket and pulled out the wallowed, pockmocked baggie of Oxy pills, then put it in Mouse's beefy palm. "Will you get rid of these?"

Mouse rolled his eyes up to meet Wes's pleading gaze. "You bet. You take care, Little Man."

The window buzzed up, then the Town Car pulled away.

Wes stood and puffed out his cheeks in an exhale. At least the Oxy was out of his life.

He turned and made his way back inside, then stuffed the books into his backpack, and went out to the tee range to let Randolph know he was ready to leave. He braced himself for more pushback from Randolph, but his dad seemed to have let the incident go.

Because he was so sure that Wes would obey?

"It'll be nice when you get your driver's license back," Randolph said when they climbed in.

"Don't I know it."

"How do you like working with Jade? Other than the obvious, of course."

"She's cool," Wes said. "Said she learned to play from her dad."

"Her father is one of the greatest card sharps of all time. Looks like she's going to follow in his footsteps."

Something which Randolph obviously admired.

"I was wrong about something, Wes."

Wes blinked. Maybe his dad was going to backtrack on the college thing.

"Chance is a decent kid. Maybe a little rough around the edges, but he's a hard worker."

Wes manufactured a little smile. "Yeah."

Randolph took a phone call, which spared him from conversation on the drive. As usual, his mind wandered to Meg and what she was doing. His chest and body ached from missing her, but he hoped she was having fun. Without him.

"I'll be back in an hour," Randolph said when he dropped him off.

"Okay."

"Oh, and Wes?"

He turned back and lifted his hand to his mouth.

"Enough with the fingernail chewing... card players should have nice hands."

Wes lowered his hand, then watched his father drive away.

He dragged himself inside and went back to the table where Jade sat shuffling decks and stacking chips, as if it were a speed game.

"Hi," he said.

"Sit down," she said without looking up.

He swung into the seat and sighed.

"What's with the long face? Did your girlfriend break up with you?"

"Not yet," he groused.

She stopped shuffling. "Do you even want to be here?"

He straightened. "Yeah... yes."

She nodded slowly. "Good... because you're a decent card player, Wes."

"Ha. If I'm so good, then how did you beat me?"

"Simple," she said. "I cheated."

He gave a little laugh. "You mean by not wearing a bra?"

"No. I mean, I cheated."

Wes's eyes sprang wide. "Seriously?"

"Seriously. That's how I won the tournament. I didn't cheat on every hand, just when I needed to."

"But that's..."

"Immoral? Bad? Dishonest?"

"Uh... yeah."

She shrugged. "It's a card game, not someone's soul." Then she scoffed. "Look, your dad is paying me a lot of money to teach you how to win. Cheating is how to win."

Wes shook his head. "I don't know..."

"Aren't you tired of the way he looks at you, man? Like you're a loser?"

So she'd noticed. "Yeah," he admitted.

"So... be a winner," she said. "I can show you how, but you have to want it."

Wes reflected on everything that had happened today... this week... this year... this life. No matter how hard he tried, he couldn't seem to catch a break. And yeah, he'd give anything to have Randolph for once look at him with something other than contempt for his bloodline.

"So show me."

‖‖‖ ‖‖‖

CHAPTER 18

"THANK YOU, Dr. Denton," Carlotta said, shaking his hand. "I thought this session was... useful, but I feel as if I have a long way to go."

"Maybe not as far as you think," he said with a warm smile. "I wish all my patients were as resilient and self-aware. Same time, next week?"

She nodded, then left his office feeling a modicum lighter. It had helped to unburden herself to someone who had no stake in the outcome of events in her life, someone she didn't have to lie to. Maybe therapy would help her to sort through all the debris in her life, and help her to move forward instead of always looking back. The therapy session seemed to have opened some kind of emotional portal, because as she walked to the train, she fell into a deep churn.

On some level, had she always suspected Randolph wasn't her real father? And would she carry a hole in her heart until she filled it with certainty?

Feeling raw, she boarded the train and found a less crowded car. Instead of sitting, she opted to stand and hold onto a pole, idly watching the news screen on the monitor above her head a few feet away. As per usual, politics was a hot topic. She was mildly tuned out until she recognized a woman who appeared on the screen—it was the redhead who was on the same flight to Dallas, the one who'd spoken to her in the security line.

This is more clothes than I took off for my date last night.

Carlotta moved closer to the monitor to read the closed caption titles.

The campaign of Presidential frontrunner
Georgia Democratic Senator Max Reeder is
being rocked by rumors of infidelity.
Colleen Mason claims she has proof of a long-
running affair with the married father of
five. More to come on this one, folks.

The segment showed Senator Reeder being dogged by
reporters. He was a tall, handsome man, who had run locally on
the platform of family values, and often featured his good-looking
wife and children in his commercials. On the screen he was
vehemently shaking his head, obviously in denial of the rumors. In
contrast Colleen Mason appeared calm standing next to her
attorney and spokesperson.

Hm. How odd to have a passing encounter with someone who
would become so newsworthy. At least it would give her
something more pleasant and anecdotal to associate with the trip
than Patricia's death.

And Jack's rejection.

CHAPTER 19

"NAME OF inmate?" the woman on the other side of the window intoned.

"Ashford," Carlotta said. "Peter Ashford."

"And your name?"

"Carlotta Wren." Then she spelled it. She knew the drill.

If someone had told her when she was a senior in high school and engaged to Peter Ashford, a handsome young man from a good family attending Vanderbilt University, that she would someday be visiting him in jail, she would've thought they were insane.

Life had dealt them both a lot of ups and downs, but this was a trench she wasn't sure Peter would be able to emerge from intact.

She signed a waiver digitally, then leaned against a dingy wall in the waiting area of the Fulton County Correctional Facility— there were no seats available. She remembered seeing a local politician make a remark about the jails being overcrowded. Perhaps the situation would help Peter's attorney to secure him bail.

She was restless during the wait. Visitors had to leave all personal items in lockers, so she couldn't even use her phone to return emails. The tasks to complete the bridal salon were piling up and although Lindy was pitching in, Carlotta was feeling overwhelmed without an assistant yet in place. She rubbed her temples in an attempt to ease the tension headache sitting there. Her nicotine patch had run out a couple of hours ago. It had been a long day, and she wasn't looking forward to this visit.

Which made her feel like a terrible person. She had signed up for the pilot texting program in the hope that she could communicate with Peter more often on a casual basis. But that had ended badly. He used to call her occasionally... but not lately. It was their last phone call that had compelled her to pay him an in-person visit.

She had attended a country club gala with Randolph, and had relished being on the arm of her celebrated father, recently exonerated and heralded a hero by the high society cohorts who had scorned him in his absence. Randolph had been in his element, basking in the attention and the power of the evening. She had excused herself to the ladies' room and received a call from Peter who, presumably knew about the event from his parents, and assumed she would be there. He had just learned he probably wouldn't get out on bail for the long wait up to a trial, and he'd sounded desperate.

Randolph isn't what you think he is.

At the time, she'd dismissed it as Peter lashing out at Randolph for being exonerated while he and the partners at Mashburn & Tully had been taken into custody for the counterfeiting Ponzi scheme. But now she wasn't so sure.

After what seemed like an eternity, her name was called and she was led in a small group to a long narrow room with a bank of phones along a Plexiglass wall. The walls had a greenish cast and the overhead lights were harsh. It was such an unpleasant place to visit, she couldn't imagine having to exist there.

She lowered herself into the hard chair of her assigned booth, and in a few minutes, Peter was led in, his hands cuffed in front of him to allow him to hold a two-way phone. She had steeled herself, but was unprepared for how much he'd changed. His lank blond hair was pulled back into a ponytail and his face was gaunt. He'd grown a scraggly beard. He seemed twitchy and nervous. But his eyes lit up when he saw her.

They both picked up their receivers. He smiled. "Hi, Carly."

She had to take a deep breath to steady her voice. "Hi, Peter. How are you?"

He nodded, but she could tell he was struggling to be upbeat. "I'm okay. Thank you for the books you sent. I've been reading a lot to pass the time."

"You're welcome."

"You are so beautiful," he said suddenly. "I hate myself for not telling you every minute we were together. The biggest mistake of my life was breaking off our first engagement. I sometimes think this is karma for the way I abandoned you."

"That's all in the past," she said. "Right now you need to concentrate all your energy on getting out of here. Do you have any news?"

"I have a new bail hearing in two weeks. My attorney is hopeful we'll get a sympathetic judge."

"Is there anything I can do to help?"

His smile was watery. "Just don't give up on me."

She smiled. "Peter, don't give up on your*self.*"

"I'm trying to be positive," he said, but his voice shook. "How are you doing, Carly?"

"I'm okay," she said, nodding. "I got a promotion at work, so I've been working a lot."

"How is your family?"

"My mother is doing well—she's much like her old self. My parents are moving to a new house."

"They're selling the Buckhead house?"

She nodded.

"An end to an era, huh? Remember when you used to climb down that tree to sneak out with me?"

She laughed. "Yes... I can't believe we never got caught."

"Me neither... Randolph would've murdered me."

"Probably." Then she angled her head and chose her words carefully. "Peter, the last time we talked, you said Randolph isn't what I think he is. What did you mean?"

His expression looked pinched. "I shouldn't have said that."

"But you did, and now I'm worried."

"You shouldn't worry, Carly. Randolph adores you, no matter what."

"No matter what?"

He wet his lips. "No matter what... happens. Or whatever... comes out."

Carlotta frowned. "What could happen? What could come out?"

He shook his head. "I've already said too much. It's not my secret to tell."

She chose her words carefully. "Whose is it?"

"Your father's."

"And my mother's?"

"I don't think even your mother knows."

Carlotta was thoroughly confused now. "Peter, just be straight with me—please."

He shook his head. "I can't, not while I'm in here. It's too dangerous. I'll tell you if I ever get out."

"Now you're scaring me."

"Stay close to Randolph. He won't let anything happen to you."

"Time's up," said the guard.

Peter cast a nervous look at the guard, then set the receiver down without saying another word. He blew her a kiss with his cuffed hands, then walked to meet a guard on his side.

Carlotta's heart was hammering when she set down the receiver on her side, trying to figure out what to make of his ramblings.

Was Peter even in his right mind?

CHAPTER 20

"WREN, YOU'RE UP!" the crow at the counter shouted.

Wes pushed himself to his feet, then walked to the counter and leaned down, extending a flower he'd picked from the landscaping on the way in. "This is my last time here, so now you and I can go out."

The woman looked up at him and glared, then grabbed the flower. "Scram."

But as he walked away, he saw her put the flower to her nose. Wes smiled, then instantly thought of Meg and how something like that would make her smile. Which instantly made him miserable. In the back of his mind, he'd known someday she'd get tired of him because she was who she was and he was something else, but he was hoping to have enough time with her to lay down some really good memories...

Dammit, he loved her.

He rubbed at the pain behind his breastbone, gave his wussy ass a pep talk, then knocked on E's door.

"Come in," she called.

He opened the door and walked in. E. Jones was sitting at her desk, moving folders around. "Come in, Wes. I have news from the D.A.'s office."

"Already?"

"Yes. Your new attorney moves fast."

He settled into the seat across from her, and found a nail to nibble.

She smiled. "So the long and short of it is, the D.A. in Clark County, Nevada agreed to turn over your sentencing to the D.A. here in Fulton County."

"Okay," he mumbled.

"Unfortunately, the D.A.'s office can't let you off with just probation. And since these are serious crimes, you'll have to pay a fine and serve significant community service hours."

"So I'm being sent back to ASS?"

"Atlanta Systems Services is such a small shop, it would take you years to work off this sentence there. You'd be better off performing your community service at a place that has evening and weekend hours so you can schedule around your regular job. Your attorney suggested doing it at one of the city golf courses."

Shit. That had Randolph written all over it. He went back to chewing.

E. leaned forward. "But an assistant D.A. and I put our heads together and made a couple of phone calls, and came up with another option you might find interesting."

He stopped chewing. "What?"

"Working for the county morgue."

His jaw dropped. "Seriously?"

She nodded. "Your friend Dr. Craft said he'd be delighted to have you there, if you're willing."

Wes dove across the desk and hugged her. She laughed, but she didn't object. "I take it that's a yes."

"Yes!" Wes shouted.

"I don't think I've ever seen someone so happy with their punishment," she said. Then she gave him a pointed look. "But you'll still have to check in with me regularly."

He nodded. "I can do that. What about the ankle bracelet?"

"That comes off."

"Awesome."

She smiled. "So we're all set. I'll get the paperwork started, your attorney will touch base, and I'll see you next week."

"Sounds good," Wes said, walking to the door with a bounce.

"Oh, Wes."

He turned back.

"Do you want to leave a urine sample?"

He grinned. "Nah. I'm clean."

She gave him a thumbs up.

Wes left her office and did a fist pump in the air. "Yes!"

He skipped back through the waiting room, stopped at the window, leaned in and kissed the old crow soundly on her lips, then kept going and jogged out into the sunshine, whooping.

Life was good again.

He was unlocking his bike and whistling under his breath when his phone rang. He didn't recognize the local number but decided to answer in case it had something to do with his sentencing.

"Hello?"

"Is this Wesley Wren?" a male voice asked.

"Yeah, who's this?"

"I'm Meg's friend, Mark. Remember me?"

The friend of Meg's brother, the preppie dude he'd seen her out with a few times before they'd started dating. He'd seen text messages from the asshat saying how much he disliked Wes—and the feeling was categorically mutual.

"Yeah, I remember. What do you want?"

"When was the last time you heard from Meg?"

"Look, dude, I know you're into her and all, but—"

"Dammit, just tell me when you last heard from her."

"It's been a week," Wes admitted. "But she's been biking with friends all over Ireland and shit, so she probably doesn't have cell service."

"She's missing."

Wes blinked. "What?"

"She's missing. Her parents haven't heard from her in days. Her friends haven't seen her. They're worried something's happened to her."

Panic squeezed his lungs, but his mind raced for an explanation. "Maybe she struck out on her own, is staying in hostels. Maybe someone stole her phone."

"Look, I hate to admit this," Mark said, "but she's head over heels for you. I don't get it, but whatever. The thing is, when her roommates started looking for her they found a piece of Meg's jewelry in a pawn shop, said she always wore it and she'd never, ever sell it. Said it was a rose gold bracelet you'd given her."

Fear like he'd never known gripped Wes's heart.

CHAPTER 21

CARLOTTA WAS sitting at her desk, fighting a yawn. She'd spent more hours at work this week than not, and the strain was wearing on her. It had taken a Herculean effort and piles of nicotine patches, but the bridal salon was on schedule and on-budget to open in the fall. When her new assistant was hired, they would go to Dallas for the training she and Patricia were supposed to have received, then all the pieces would be in place.

Every time she looked at the renderings for the shop, she was filled with pride and excitement that the project had been entrusted to her, and she'd delivered.

Plus ten points.

From the corner of her desk, her cell phone rang, and she was surprised to see Jack's name come up on the screen—and pleased her heart hadn't turned over like a puppy wanting its belly rubbed.

"Hi, Jack."

"Hi, Carlotta. Is this a bad time?"

"No, this is a good time, actually. I'm done for the day except for a wrap-up meeting in fifteen minutes."

"This won't take that long. I just received a call from Detective Lawson in Dallas. Patricia Alexander's death has been ruled an accident. Looks like you're off the hook."

She put her phone between her neck and shoulder and reached for her tote bag. "Okay, thanks for letting me know."

"That's good news, isn't it?"

"Yes, of course." She opened her bag and unzipped an inner pocket.

"So... it ends here. You're not going to keep chasing this?"

"No, Jack." She pulled out the plastic baggie containing the used condom she'd found in Patricia's bathroom.

He made a dubious noise. "Why don't I believe you?"

She held it up to the light and studied it. "Because you're a very suspicious person."

"Uh-huh. Well, there was another reason I called."

At the serious tone in his voice, she stowed the baggie and refocused. "I'm listening."

"I… I just want to say that Coop is a lucky guy. To have you in his life."

She bit into her lip. "That's nice of you to say."

"I mean it. You're… special. You deserve someone like Coop."

"I believe so, too," she said earnestly. "Coop makes me happy."

"Then that makes me happy."

"Good—everyone's happy." She cleared her throat. "So… how's the reorg going in the department?"

"Better than I thought," he admitted. "Because of the arrests in the Mashburn & Tully case, I'll be liaising with the GBI on future cases… all roads seems to lead back to you, Carlotta."

She laughed. "I'm not sure how to take that."

"Take it as a compliment."

"Okay, I will." She checked her watch. "I have to run, Jack. Thanks for calling."

"Sure. Tell Prissy hi for me."

"Will do."

She ended the call and waited for the predictable pang of regret to pierce her heart… but happily, it didn't.

Smiling to herself, she gathered up the latest renderings for the salon and other items she needed for her meeting with Lindy. She took her tote bag since she intended to leave right after the meeting. It would feel good to get home at a decent hour to hang with Wes. Maybe she'd give Coop a call and they'd make a pizza.

At Lindy's office, her assistant gave Carlotta a nod, accustomed to seeing her for the weekly wrap-up. Carlotta rapped on Lindy's open door.

Lindy lifted her head, then smiled. "Come in. It's been a hectic week."

"Yes," Carlotta agreed, setting the thick portfolio in a chair. "But I have good news. HR made an offer to Quentin Gallagher which he accepted, so he can start right away. I'd like to reschedule the Dallas training trip as soon as possible." She lowered herself into a chair, and lifted a smile to her boss.

But it wasn't returned. Lindy folded her hands on the top of her spotless desk. "I'm afraid I have some bad news, Carlotta. The bridal salon project has been scrapped."

Carlotta blinked. "Scrapped? Is this a joke?"

"I wish."

Her mind reeled. "All the work, all the planning... for nothing?"

Lindy's expression was stoic. "The decision is no reflection on you, Carlotta. You've done everything that was asked of you and more... and under difficult circumstances. This restructuring move came from the highest level, even I wasn't in the loop. I found out less than an hour ago. I'm as disappointed as you are."

Carlotta gave a little laugh. "I doubt that."

"Fair enough." Lindy sighed. "Of course, that means your position has been eliminated along with the project."

That thought hadn't yet occurred to her—another blow. "Is there another director's job available?"

"Unfortunately, no." Then Lindy smiled. "But you can have your old job back. That's where your greatest strengths lie—on the sales floor. And as soon as an opportunity becomes available, you'll be considered for it. How's that sound?"

Carlotta studied the woman who represented the place where she'd spent most of her adult life. She'd earned a decent living, but she'd worked hard for it, and somewhere along the way, she'd come to believe she wasn't qualified to do anything else. Patricia's words came back to her.

I think you could do whatever you set your mind to.

A quiet calm seeped over her. "I quit." Carlotta reached up to remove her nameplate from her jacket, then set it on Lindy's desk.

Lindy looked incredulous. "Don't do this, Carlotta."

"I already did."

"But... what are you going to do?"

"Anything I want."

Carlotta picked up her bag, then turned around and walked out of the administrative offices, onto the sales floor, and rode down the escalator. She felt utterly serene, yet underneath a river of excitement bubbled in her veins.

Already the world seemed bigger, brighter, and lying at her well-shod feet.

As she walked toward the nearest train station, her phone rang, displaying a Dallas, Texas number. Carlotta connected the call. "Hello?"

"Is this Carlotta Wren?"

"Yes."

"This is the Saxler House hotel in Dallas, Texas. I'm calling to let you know a cell phone was found belonging to a guest named Patricia Alexander. There's a note in Lost and Found to contact you?"

Carlotta gripped her phone harder. "Yes. And you're sure it's the correct phone?"

"Her initials are on the case, ma'am."

"I see. Ms. Alexander was a coworker of mine. I need to check it for proprietary business files, then I'll make sure her family receives it." She gave her address. "May I ask where the phone was found?"

"It was under the trash dumpster, ma'am. I'm afraid the screen has been damaged."

"I'm just relieved you found it. Thank you for following up."

Carlotta ended the call, pondering the timing of the universe, and choosing to take it as a sign.

As she walked, she mulled the information Coop had given her on DNA kits and online family trees. If she could have the fluid in the condom tested and posted to one of those sites, she might be able to track down John Smythe or tie it back to the taxi stand guy. Pulling it off anonymously wouldn't be easy, but if nothing else, her short stint in management had upped her technical skills.

Starting at the end, in her mind she backtracked and looped forward, thinking of all the ways she might be exposed, and how to circumvent detection at each step.

At the next ATM, she withdrew three hundred dollars in small bills. Then she stopped at a pharmacy and used the cash to purchase a generic debit gift card. Further down the street she stopped off at an upscale hotel and breezed by the front desk to ask for directions to the business center. Because of the way she was dressed, no one questioned her status as a guest. In fact, the clerk offered her a bottle of water, which she accepted.

At the business center, she signed on to one of the public computers used to print boarding passes, and set up a disposable email account with fake contact information that was gender neutral. Then she accessed a big-box shopping site to purchase a DNA kit under the throwaway email address using the fake name and paid with the debit gift card. For the ship-to address, she decided she needed a place where lots of people received mail, so she chose a co-working space in a busy part of town. Before she completed the purchase, she replayed the steps in her head to make sure she'd thought of everything.

And as she stared at the description of the DNA kit, another thought slid into her mind.

She could have her own DNA tested and posted anonymously... and perhaps find her biological father.

With a single keystroke, she changed the quantity of kits from one to two.

The worst kind of lie, Carlotta decided, were the lies she told herself. Because, dammit, she did want to know where she came from.

She hit the Submit Order button, then cleared the browsing history, and signed off. Sipping from the complimentary bottle of water, she casually walked back through the hotel lobby and out onto the crowded sidewalk.

Plus ten points.

-The End-

A NOTE FROM THE AUTHOR

Thank you so very much for reading 10 BODIES LYING!

So what did you think about the theme for this book? Did it make you think about how everyone lies? I confess it made me evaluate how often I tell lies thinking I'm protecting someone's feelings or circumventing a bigger problem. But have you ever been caught in a lie... or been lied to? There are so many uncomfortable emotions wrapped up in lies. In this book Carlotta is starting to examine lies she's been told, and lies she's believed about herself, such as she's not capable of doing anything more than what she's always done. I hope I achieved some of those things and made you want to keep reading. Rest assured I'll be continuing the Body Movers series—I'll keep writing as long you keep coming along for the ride!

A shout-out to the following readers for entering my Facebook title contest and submitting the title I ultimately used for this book:

Francine Curtis, St. Paul, MN	Melissa Lonergan, West Deptford, NJ
Janice Tatrow, Holland, MI	Cindy Rosenberg, South Pasadena, CA
Jenna Crance, Rahway, NJ	Sally Pauls Garand, Augusta, ME
Gwen Hansen, Concord, NC	Holly Pirtle, Laurel, MD
Nadine Nevland, Toronto, ON	Lisa Foss, Middletown, RI
Sharon Hall, Jacksonville, FL	

Thanks so much, everyone!

If you enjoyed 10 BODIES LYING and you have a few minutes to leave an Amazon review, I would appreciate it very much. Online bookstores use reviews as a factor for showing a book to readers when they're browsing. Attracting new readers means I can keep writing new stories! (I'd like to write at least two more titles in the BODY MOVERS series.) Plus I always want to know what my readers are thinking. Are you on Team Jack, Team Coop, or Team Peter? Or do you think Carlotta should explore other options? Do you have feelings about what should happen with some of the other characters?

And are you signed up to receive notices of my future book releases? If not, please visit www.stephaniebond.com and enter your email address. I won't flood you with emails and I'll never share or sell your address, and you can unsubscribe at any time. While you're on my website, check out the FAQs page for more information about the history and the future of the Body Movers series.

Thanks again for your time and interest, and for telling your friends about my books. As long as you keep reading, I'll keep writing!

Happy reading!

Stephanie Bond

OTHER WORKS BY STEPHANIE BOND

Humorous romantic mysteries:
COMEBACK GIRL—*Home is where the hurt is.*
TEMP GIRL—*Change is good... but not great.*
COMA GIRL—*You can learn a lot when people think you aren't listening.*
TWO GUYS DETECTIVE AGENCY—*Even Victoria can't keep a secret from us...*
OUR HUSBAND—*Hell hath no fury like three women scorned!*
KILL THE COMPETITION—*There's only one sure way to the top...*
I THINK I LOVE YOU—*Sisters share everything in their closets...including the skeletons.*
GOT YOUR NUMBER—*You can run, but your past will eventually catch up with you.*
WHOLE LOTTA TROUBLE—*They didn't plan on getting caught...*
IN DEEP VOODOO—*A woman stabs a voodoo doll of her ex, and then he's found murdered!*
VOODOO OR DIE—*Another voodoo doll, another untimely demise...*
BUMP IN THE NIGHT—*a short mystery*

***Body Movers* series:**
PARTY CRASHERS (full-length prequel)
BODY MOVERS
2 BODIES FOR THE PRICE OF 1
3 MEN AND A BODY
4 BODIES AND A FUNERAL
5 BODIES TO DIE FOR
6 KILLER BODIES
6 ½ BODY PARTS (novella)
7 BRIDES FOR SEVEN BODIES
8 BODIES IS ENOUGH
9 BODIES ROLLING
10 BODIES LYING

Romances:
FACTORY GIRL—*Long hours, low pay, and big dreams.*
DIAMOND MINE—*A woman helps her beloved choose a ring—for another woman!*
SEEKING SINGLE MALE (for the holidays)—*A singles ad mixup leads to mistletoe mayhem!*
TAKING CARE OF BUSINESS—*An FBI agent goes undercover at a Vegas wedding chapel to nab a mobster and gets all shook up instead!*
MANHUNTING IN MISSISSIPPI—*If you can't stand the heat, get back in bed...*
ALMOST A FAMILY—*Fate gave them a second chance at love...*
LICENSE TO THRILL—*She's between a rock and a hard body...*
STOP THE WEDDING!—*If anyone objects to this wedding, speak now...*
THREE WISHES—*Be careful what you wish for!*

The Southern Roads series:
BABY, I'M YOURS (novella)
BABY, DRIVE SOUTH
BABY, COME HOME
BABY, DON'T GO
BABY, I'M BACK (novella)
BABY, HOLD ON (novella)
BABY, IT'S YOU (novella)

Nonfiction:
GET A LIFE! 8 STEPS TO CREATE YOUR OWN LIFE LIST—*a short how-to for mapping out your personal life list!*
YOUR PERSONAL FICTION-WRITING COACH: *365 Days of Motivation & Tips to Write a Great Book!*

ABOUT THE AUTHOR

Stephanie Bond was seven years deep into a corporate career in computer programming and pursuing an MBA at night when an instructor remarked she had a flair for writing and suggested she submit material to academic journals. But Stephanie was more interested in writing fiction—more specifically, romance and mystery novels. After writing in her spare time for two years, she sold her first manuscript; after selling ten additional projects to two publishers, she left her corporate job to write fiction full-time. To-date, Stephanie has more than eighty published novels to her name, including the popular BODY MOVERS humorous mystery series, and STOP THE WEDDING!, a romantic comedy adapted into a movie for the Hallmark Channel. Stephanie lives in Atlanta, where she is probably working on a story at this very moment. For more information on Stephanie's books, visit www.stephaniebond.com.

COPYRIGHT INFORMATION

Made in the
USA
Columbia, SC